Second
CHRISTMAS

Second
CHRISTMAS

HOLLY KNIGHTLEY

ISBN: 978-1-958761-75-5

Cover design: Marshmallow Designs

For Gimply

CONTENTS

CHAPTER ONE

The Man with the Birthmark

I hate Christmas. So much so, they should put it on my tombstone when I die. Cookie Marlowe: She hated Christmas. Bah humbug!

I can't help it! When the weather starts to turn sour and there's a hum of Christmas melodies in the air, my stomach twists into a knot—into one big figurative red bow that, if I was disemboweled, could be used to top a brand-new bike for some soon to be mortified kid—macabre family Christmas done right.

Urgh, the stores are playing Christmas music earlier and earlier. I heard *Santa Claus is Coming to Town* in Walmart back in September and broke into a cold sweat. I turned the aisle and was face to face with mini-Santa Clauses, each of their beady eyes twinkling at me, their plump, rosy-cheeked faces painted in a knowing smile. Oh, he knows who's naughty or nice, alright. Together, standing there as a fleet of Santas, I could only guess what else they knew. I was sure they saw right through my bah humbug attitude—that's a hell yes. Scratch that—*ho* yes.

It's not that I was on the naughty list or had a personal vendetta against the fat man in the red suit. Or that I found the holiday too commercialized or stressful. If I was being candid, which I was from time to time—there was something about the cold of winter that kept me honest—I would acknowledge my hatred for the holiday stemmed from fear, as so often hate does. I was another cliché, way worse than the mock holiday spirit you can buy in a bottle and spray on your faux Christmas tree.

It all started when I was ten. I remember because that year for my birthday I had asked my big brother, Jax, for a real Christmas tree. It didn't matter that my birthday wasn't until mid-January, I called in my birthday order. Back then, Christmas was my favorite holiday, and we always had an artificial tree, despite that every year I asked for a real one. As an adult, I understand the complications with my request. I lived with my brother in a third-floor apartment. It used to be the four of us, my mother, father, brother and me—then it was the three of us after my stepfather, Red, died. Then it was just the two of us.

Jaxson was younger than I am now—twenty-two—when Mom left and didn't come back. It wasn't long after Red's accident. It was blow after blow that year. The ground had been painted white since Thanksgiving, and everyone already had their Christmas lights up and I vividly imagined their stockings were hung by the chimney with care. Everyone was preparing for a merry Christmas—everyone that was, but us. I think Jaxson said yes to the real tree to try to cheer me up about Mom leaving. Now that I recall it, I think he answered my letter to Santa that year.

At the time, I still believed in Santa. I was one of the few in my class who did. How could I not? We were poor—always had been—yet I always got what I wanted on my Christmas list. There was only one way to explain it—Santa. And I knew that year as I sat down to pen my letter to Old Saint Nick that it would be no different; he would bring me exactly what I asked for.

I can still recall my laser focus all those years ago, my brow furrowing, beads of concentration gathering in my hair line as I meticulously wrote each letter perfectly, so there could be no mistake in knowing what I wanted for Christmas. I had asked my brother for a real tree, but what I asked Santa for was nothing short of a Christmas miracle: Please bring me a new family that is perfect and will love me forever and ever.

Santa came through. Jaxson changed that Christmas, stepping up to the plate and becoming mom, dad, and brother all in one and I didn't have to wait until Christmas morning for my miracle. Thanks to Santa, he was more than willing to get me a Christmas tree for an early birthday present.

As we got out of his truck at Kip's Tree Farm over a decade ago, I had breathed in the cold air, letting it fill my lungs until I thought I would burst with Christmas spirit. There had never been a kid that enjoyed Christmas more than me. How I had laughed, and so had Jaxson. He always did when I acted silly. I had snorted the pine aroma, thinking I'd never been happier. I didn't need my mother; I had Jaxson, and we were getting a *real* tree. I knew it would be the best Christmas ever! Despite it all, this would be a Christmas to remember.

I can still recall the overwhelming feeling of joy at taking my brother's hand as I dragged him into the hustle and bustle of the tree farm, my eyes as wide as saucers as I tried to take everything in at the same time. The trees at the entrance greeted us with the glitz and glam befitting Christmas trees, their colorful ornaments shining along with the colored lights that twinkled like winking faeries beckoning us closer. As we entered, trees flanked us on both sides, pulling my attention each way, my head going back and forth in a tug-of-war.

There was one decorated exclusively in silver and gold like the song from *Rudolph the Red-Nosed Reindeer* and one decked out in every color of the rainbow. Jaxson had really liked the Christmas tree decorated with different beer cans hanging from bright red ribbons. My favorite had pinecones dipped in peanut butter with birdseed sprinkled on it like nature's glitter. We had made those in school, and I had hung mine on the balcony of the apartment for the birds. This tree didn't stop with peanut butter and birdseed covered pinecones; there were plenty of other delicious delicacies to be enjoyed by the woodland creatures that called Kip's Tree Farm home. Dried fruit festooned the large tree in sweeping swags, perfuming the air with apples and oranges while dried apricots, with smiley faces constructed from raisins, hung proudly from thick sprigs. It was perfect. I imagined Santa would leave the Christmas gifts for the tree farm's furry residents under this tree just like he had in the *Frosty the Snowman* cartoon.

Oh God, how I had tugged on Jaxson's arm begging him to take me back to Kip's on Christmas Eve so we could have cocoa with squirrels and rabbits and the wild turkeys. He didn't say no, and that made my smile radiate from my eyes. I can still feel the love that glazed over them that day—this all-encompassing, grateful love. I was sure I must have looked like a child-shaped Christmas tree.

As we walked deeper into the tree farm, my eyes had danced around like a sugar plum fairy. Lights were strung up above us, sparkling like stars in daylight. There was a concession stand selling hot cocoa and refreshments. The smell of chocolate and cinnamon had washed over me like a sugary dream, making my mouth water. This craving for all things Christmas was further amplified by the music blaring from large speakers wearing their very own Santa hats. I had found myself humming along to *Santa Claus is Coming to Town,* just as I spotted the sign for Santa. I was so excited, I couldn't hold still. I wiggled like I had ants in my pants and that's when I realized, like all children who ignore it until they can't, I had to pee.

Santa would have to wait. There was a small co-ed bathroom with a few stalls not far from the parking lot. My brother had waited for me outside when I rushed in. I was going to make this as quick as humanly possible. Every second I was in the bathroom was a second I was missing something Christmassy. I yanked the toilet paper off the roll hurriedly, creating a bathroom tissue nest over the toilet seat just the way my mother had taught me before I sat down. I was still humming along to the music in my head when I heard the door to the bathroom open.

The person who entered came right up to the stall I was in, and for a moment I thought they were going to try to open the door. I wasn't worried, I had locked it. My mother had taught me to always lock the bathroom door, and I always did what she said because I wanted to be on Santa's nice list. That close to Christmas, I wasn't taking any chances.

It's always embarrassing when you tug on the door to find out the stall is occupied, so I was about to say, 'I'm in here' when my attention was drawn to the ground, more specifically to two large, black boots that took a step closer to my stall. The boots were scuffed, like they were old work boots. Jaxson had a few pairs that were that old. I didn't say a word and the person didn't try the stall handle. It was as if we were in some silent standoff. They just stood in front of the stall, only the toes of their worn, dusty boots visible to me and their shadow, that I could just see fanning off on an angle away from the light overhead.

My eyes had remained glued to the boots, waiting for the owner's next move. They didn't move, but their shadow did. It happened so fast, in the blink of an eye. Their shadow stretched under the bathroom stall, darkening the tiled floor in the shape of two hands. Each of the shadow's ten fingers were distinctive, long, and reaching, surging toward me like inky claws. I went to scream but my voice got trapped in my throat. Nothing came out, not even a peep. I yanked my feet up with such force I almost fell into the toilet bowl, my hands clasping the toilet seat with white knuckles, saving me from an embarrassing plummet into the *Bog of Eternal Stench.* My heart beat so loudly in my chest, I prayed Jaxson would hear it and rush in.

The shadow hands retracted just as quickly as they had reached for me. Wide-eyed, I watched the boots disappear and heard the sound of the stall door next to me open. I seized the moment and darted out of the bathroom, not taking the time to wash my hands. In a panic that spread over me like a fever, I threw open the exit door and ran straight into a boy. Our heads clapped together in a deafening clunk, nausea rising from my already upset stomach.

"Are you alright?" he had asked. Silent tears were already streaming down my face. He rubbed his temple with a gloved hand. I had assumed he was about my age as he was my height. "I'm, sorry. I didn't mean to hurt you," he'd apologized, his voice growing worried as an onslaught of sobs broke through the barrier in my throat.

I didn't respond; I wasn't crying because of him and didn't have time to explain it. I needed Jaxson. My eyes went to where I'd left him, but he wasn't there.

"Hey, I'm really sorry about your head," the boy had told me, patting my shoulder. "Don't cry. My head hurts too."

While I attempted to croak out Jaxson's name, I heard my brother's voice. "Cookie."

Spotting Jaxson in the crowd, I made a beeline for him, wrapping my arms around his waist in a death grip. Glancing back in the direction of the bathroom, I noticed the boy I had collided with was staring at me, a puzzled look fixed on his face. Just then, a man in a red plaid coat exited the restroom. It was him—I recognized the black boots. The man from the bathroom with the shadow hands was the boy's father. They were both looking in my direction now. I buried my face in my brother's coat, wishing they would go away, wishing I never saw them.

But I would never forget that boy or his father. They had the same birthmark. It was under their left eye. It was bright red and scalloped, like someone had shot them with a paint ball gun in the face. And they had silver eyes—not gray—but silver, as if their eyes weren't eyes at all, but something more.

We had left Kip's that day without a tree. That was fine with me. I didn't want a tree anymore and I never wanted to go back to Kip's Tree Farm as long as I lived, but that didn't matter—I brought the nightmare home with me.

That night the man from the bathroom visited me in my bedroom. He was next to my bed, wearing the same red plaid coat he had on at the tree farm, crouching so our faces were close. His strange steely eyes seemed to absorb and scatter the scanty light coming in through the blinds. I couldn't make out his pupils. All I could see were two silver globes. His eyes were bright—glowing—in my dark room like twin metallic moons, casting their own hazy glow on the features of his face: his paint splatter birthmark, his sloping nose, his manicured five-o'clock shadow.

I'd felt his cold breath on my cheeks, saw it as it escaped his lips in hazy phantoms that danced the Nutcracker Suite over my chin before vanishing. The smell of apples and oranges from Kip's Tree Farm skated in on his breath, but there was a hint of something else, something gone bad. It tainted my memory of my favorite tree at Kip's.

The reality that this stranger wasn't made of dried fruit, but something acrid, took a moment to sink in. When it did, when my groggy brain realized this man wasn't part of a nightmare but was *really* in my room, next to my bed, breathing his rotting breath on my face, my chest heaved. It went up and down so fast and so hard the ache was felt in my entire body. It was as if my heart was trying to power my limbs which refused to budge. I couldn't move an inch. It was like I was buried in one of those festive Jello molds made with fruit cocktail. Suspended where I lay, I was nothing more than a gelatin asphyxiated grape, soft in the center—afraid.

All I could do was move my eyes. Instinctively, they darted around the room looking for help—for like my body, my voice box had also seized. I couldn't scream and wasn't sure how I was breathing—but I was. My breath raced out of my mouth like I was a train, like I was the freaking *Polar Express*. I watched it rise above my face in a desperate S.O.S. before it vanished into the shadows, my silent call for help unanswered.

From the corner of my eye, I stared at the man, succumbing to my fate. I knew deep down inside no one was coming to help me. He smiled then, the corners of his lips twisting unnaturally upward, stretching his face until his birthmark cracked. The sound that accompanied the fault line that now zigzagged through his ruddy blemish made me think of the hollow tinkling a glass ornament makes when it falls off a Christmas tree and breaks.

From the central crack, little ones, like spider lace, shot across his cheek. He was breaking—piece by little piece he was coming apart—but there was no blood, not one drip-drop. Something about that terrified me more than if there had been an entire bathtub of blood. Blood would have been normal.

I had tried to scream again, tried to call out for Jaxson, but I couldn't. I couldn't make my tongue or lips move, but I could taste. As if my worst nightmare had been answered, the coppery tang of pennies found its way into my mouth, and I knew it was blood.

A new panic had coursed through me, unsure of where the blood was coming from. My chest had inflated and deflated with renewed vigor, pumping blood to my frenzied brain. I realized it had to be my own blood I was tasting, as it was clearly not the man's. A light bulb went off in my head. It had to be from my nose, and I was making things worse. Choking, as it welled in my mouth, I had no choice but to swallow it.

With a lone fingernail, the man had scraped at the crack in

his birthmark, each deliberate drag of his nail down his cheek sounding like a knife's edge on glass. The sound over and over again made me feel like I was being poisoned from the ear inward, in some twisted form of torture. With every fragment of his skin that chipped away from his face as if he was nothing more than a broken ornament, his skin an illusion—a fragile shell, I felt like a piece of me was lost too. Like I would never be whole again.

I had wanted to look away, after the first fleck of skin fell from his face, but I no longer had the ability to move my eyes. I couldn't close them either—they had fallen prisoner to the same strange paralysis the rest of my body had already succumbed to. Tears though—they flowed, unhindered by the spell I had found myself under. I had felt them as they rolled down the side of my face as blood continued to coat my lips, worming its way onto my tongue and collecting in the pit of my throat.

There was something under his birthmark, another skin. It was black and blue and bruised and so very ugly. So very, very ugly, and I wondered if it was the shadow I'd glimpsed in the bathroom.

The man had been handsome. I knew it to be true even when I was little, just like a child would acknowledge someone was old or young, fat or thin. Now that I recall him, I can say with certainty that the man had indeed been very handsome. However, with his face destroyed by a rictus grin, his skin cracking and chipping off like a *Humpty Dumpty* from Hell, he was nothing short of horrifying. There was something worse about it in knowing he had once been handsome. It made his transformation that much more wrong—that much more terrifying—more so than the reaching shadow in the bathroom, even if that was what was behind his eggshell skin. A shadow is a shadow and can't exist in the light, but this man was in my room. He was real.

Suddenly, the spell was broken. I could move. I had shot up in bed, my hand going to cradle my nose, where warm blood sprang from it, dripping through my trembling fingers. The man with the birthmark was gone and I knew that it had been his presence that had kept me glued in place. All at once, every fear that had been corked inside of me while the man chipped away at his face came out in one blood-curdling scream.

Jaxson had bolted into my room, still dressed, his boots scuffing the floor as he darted to my bedside. Placing his hand over mine, he had told me, "It's just a nosebleed, Cookie. Just a silly old nosebleed."

He had scooped me up in his arms and took me into the bathroom, where he placed me on the sink top. With a hand towel, he had gently dabbed at my bloody nose. "It's okay. I get them too this time of year. The cold chaps everything, even your nose. Think about all of the nosebleeds Santa must get."

I had tried to sniff in and was met with a burning sensation that traveled from my nostrils to my brain, bringing forth a new fury of sobs.

"It's okay. Let it out, don't sniff in."

I had seen the worry in his eyes that night, saw how his face was drained of color. This wasn't about me anymore, this was about him. I had scared Jaxson, probably just as much as my unwanted visitor had scared me. Jaxson was all I had left in the world and even at my young age, I'd realized how much he meant to me. I made a promise to my brother that night while the blood snaked down my lips. I promised him that I would never scare him again. The promise was made official in the only way my ten-year-old self could notarize it—by a pinky swear.

Till this day, I have kept that promise to my brother. I didn't tell Jaxson when the man came to my room the next night, his face cracking under the stress of an impossibly wide smile as he kept me pinned to the bed while he chipped away at his face and my nose bled into my mouth, choking me. I didn't mention it to him the night after that when the same thing happened again, or the next night, or the night after that. The man with the birthmark had visited me every night until New Years that year and after that, he was gone and so was my love for Christmas.

CHAPTER TWO

Return to Kip's Tree Farm

It had been four years since I made the trek home for Christmas. My holidays spent in my cramped dorm at Texas A&M University didn't feel like the holidays at all, which in part I was grateful for; nonetheless, part of me would always miss the wonder of Christmas that could only be visited through childhood memories long since passed. Passed—but not buried. I recall with a warm heart how I'd earnestly penned my letters to Santa every year, just as I would never forget the feeling of my heart being wrenched out of my chest at Kip's Tree Farm.

I had felt the temperature plummet as I inched closer to home. Having graduated a semester early thanks to taking summer classes, I was ahead of the rat race and was looking forward to seeing Jaxson and reestablishing my roots. *Zoom* calls were a far cry away from the real thing, and he'd been urging me to come home since I first left.

Jaxson didn't understand my desire to leave home. How could he? I never told him. A promise is a promise, and I had pinky-swore. Every year that I kept my little secret from him, the more I felt I had to. Yet at the same time, with every year that went by, with the addition of the miles and miles between me and my hometown, the episode in the bathroom seemed trivial, and I was able to see it for what it was: the overactive imagination of a scared little girl.

I had my bachelor's in psychology now and, sure, I needed a master's degree to do anything with my very expensive slip of paper; still, I had learned a few things along the way. Trauma, whether it be childhood trauma or not, affects everyone differently. It wasn't surprising that with my stepfather's death, followed by my mother ditching Jaxson and me, that I was manifesting signs of post-traumatic stress disorder, imagining a shadow reaching for me and the man the shadow belonged to visiting my bedroom at night.

To make a bad situation worse, Jaxson hadn't been immediately keen on raising me, adding to my fear of being abandoned. I had spent sleepless nights in anticipation of his decision to let me stay with him or be placed in a foster home. It was this fear that had spurred my desperate plea for Santa to bring me a new family.

Thankfully, I didn't have to wait long for my Christmas miracle. That very night, Jaxson had wrapped me in a bear hug as we watched *Frosty Returns* on TV. I can still remember what he whispered in my ear like it was yesterday: "I'm never letting you go. I will make your Christmas wish come true one way or another, my little Sugar Cookie."

I no longer believed in Santa. That naive little girl grew up a long time ago. I could see my situation for what it was, with the eyes of an adult. Jaxson had made my Christmas wish come true. He had made good on his promise the next day by taking me to Kip's, and we know how that turned out. The truth of the situation was that I had been thrilled to be getting a real tree, but at the same time I was horribly unhappy. My mother should have been taking me, not Jaxson. I could say I didn't need her, but that was a big fat lie that Santa of make-believe could see right through. Every little girl needs her mother, especially at Christmas.

The man with the birthmark and the shadow hands was a

roadblock that I made to stop myself from enjoying Christmas. I was punishing myself for things that were out of my control and weren't my fault. Red had died and my mother had left—that was not my burden to bear.

I wasn't a little girl anymore and I wasn't going to let my dead-beat mother ruin another Christmas. My mother made her choice to cut and run after Red passed away and now *I* was making a choice. This year, I was taking my life back and I was starting by getting the biggest, fattest, Christmas tree Kip's Tree Farm had to offer. After all, I never did get my birthday Christmas tree that year and it was time to rectify that. I couldn't believe that I let one scary incident in a bathroom when I was ten years old, and incidentally a few scary nights, flip my world upside down and turn a holiday I loved into a dreadful time of year. I was feeling murderous. I was going to kill my childhood fear, and I was taking the head-on approach, cutting it off by the trunk—the tree trunk, that is.

But as Jaxson drove into the parking lot of Kip's, I felt my resolve turn into butter. It was as if my body had liquefied just like *Frosty the Snowman*'s had when he met his demise in the greenhouse at the hands of the conniving magician. I was nothing more than a pile of gooey organs caked into the seat cushion along with all of the other unidentified grime that had been there since I was a kid.

"You sure you can handle this?" Jaxson asked with weary eyes. "Because we don't have to get a tree, you know that, right?" He looked tired, older than the last time I saw him, as if *Zoom* had smoothed the fine lines around his eyes and forehead, keeping him forever as I remembered him.

I feigned a smile. "I'm sure, I'm sure, and we do need a tree. If we don't have a tree, where is Santa going to leave my gifts?" I asked playfully, flicking my light brown hair off my shoulders. "I've been very good this year. The very best, in fact. I don't want to give the fat man any excuses. I want a big-screen TV."

Jaxson lit up, his cheeks alive with a winter glow that kept my pseudo smile plastered to my face. I felt like a butterfly that just had its wings pinned down in a bug collection. All I wanted to do was close my wings and hide, but I couldn't, so I kept smiling.

I wasn't sure what Jaxson thought after my meltdown all those years ago. Maybe he thought I hated Christmas because of Red's death or my mother leaving, or maybe a combination of both.

I can still recall the disapproving faces of the strangers as they stared while I sobbed hysterically, stamping my feet in a tantrum. Their reproachful looks had swarmed around me until their faces were all blank blurs, but in my haze of salty tears I could still see the bright eyes of the boy with the birthmark and his father.

When we made it back to the apartment and I finally settled down, I concocted a believable lie, explaining to Jaxson that I hadn't realized that all the Christmas trees for sale were dead, and I didn't want to kill anyone else. I exploited Red's death, a thing I will always feel guilty for, but the last thing I wanted to do was give Jaxson a reason to put me in a foster home and explaining that a shadow tried to grab me was a sure way of finding myself very alone forever.

Jaxson had just kissed my forehead and called me by my pet name and said, "Sugar Cookie, you didn't kill anyone, and you never will."

His words had reduced me to sobs. He didn't blame me for Red's accident, but it was hard not to blame myself when I knew my mother did. I knew I was the reason she left us.

"Come on, Sugar Cookie," Jaxson coaxed, opening my car door and tearing me from my thoughts of the past. He took me by both hands. "Hurry, before all of the good ones are gone."

I let him pull me out of my seat, the cold air seizing my nostrils in a déjà vu moment. The smell of evergreens was like a memory from a dream. It made me smile, despite the feeling I had just left my stomach in my seat. Still, I could feel excitement sparking at the core of me, rejuvenating my body and soul from the inside out. This was just what I needed. My excitement rose with every inhale of fresh country air and was about to spill over in a titter of joy when I saw him.

It was him, the man from the bathroom—the man that had visited me in my room. He hadn't aged a day. He looked exactly how he had when I was a little girl. He even had on the same red plaid coat, the same blue jeans, the same scuffed-up boots. His chiseled face was framed with the same five-o'clock shadow that, back then, I would have called whiskers. The birthmark was unmistakable. It was so distinctive that I didn't know where to focus my attention—on it or on his eyes that were too steely to be called anything but silver. It was a sunny winter day, and yet those strange eyes glistened like a cat's at night.

I sat back down in my seat, making my body as heavy as I could while I stared straight ahead, refusing to look in the direction of the man with the birthmark. Jaxson gave me another tug.

"Let's go with an artificial tree," I suggested, doing my best to keep my cool, but I swore I could feel the man's silver eyes on me. It was as if they radiated their own heat.

"I checked; they have balled trees. We can plant our tree in the backyard after Christmas. Rest assured Sugar Cookie, you aren't killing anything."

I risked a glance toward the entrance to the tree farm again, locking eyes with the man who had scared me into hating Christmas. My breath caught as if the air was zapped out of my lungs. I inhaled sharply, forcing the cold to fill me with an ache as my heart spluttered in my chest in an irregular heartbeat.

"I want one of those pink aluminum trees from *Charlie Brown*," I bleated. "I've gone commercial."

He smiled at that, seemingly not noticing the panic attack

waging war in my mind.

"Pink aluminum tree it is, but next year I get to pick the color."

CHAPTER THREE
Return of the Nightmare

I crawled into my childhood bed, happy to be home. It was true that I didn't face my fear at Kip's, but I still made progress. It had been nearly fifteen years since Jaxson and I had a Christmas tree. True, it wasn't a real Douglas fir or an aluminum tree, but we did find a pale pink artificial Christmas tree at Walmart which we decorated with black, glittery balls. It screamed 1950's and I loved it. I don't think Jaxson was as smitten with our throwback Christmas tree, but he faked it for me.

I knew our pink tree was a far cry from the biggest, fattest Christmas tree Kip's Tree Farm had to offer, but there was always next year. I'd have no choice but to march myself right into Kip's if that was what Jaxson wanted. Maybe that was what I needed—for it to be something for him and not for myself.

I knew the man with the birthmark wasn't really there. He was a gatekeeper, stopping me from moving forward. My brain put him there as a roadblock today to test me, and I failed epically. But for Jaxson, I wouldn't. I wished I could face my fear for myself, but there was this pit of guilt inside of me that had calcified a long time ago and I knew it could never heal.

No matter how many times I told myself I wasn't to blame for Red's death and my mother leaving, there was this small part of me, right below the surface just like the face hiding behind the man's birthmark, that didn't believe it. That dark, ugly part of me felt like I was getting exactly what I deserved. Why should I have a nice Christmas when my stepfather was rotting away in a stinking grave? Why should I get to be the happy one in all of this when I was the one who had divided the family forever?

My mom had only been married to Red for two years when my stepfather's vehicle slid on black ice, sending it sailing over the guardrail of a small bridge and into the river. He had been on his way to pick me up from my Girl Scout meeting at the school. My mother had thought Girl Scouts was a big waste of time, saying that these days it was all about selling. But I had begged and whined until I got my way. If I had just listened to my mother, Red would still be alive.

I missed Red—a nickname he earned on account of his height. He had seemed as tall as a redwood tree, but he was never scary. He was the nicest person in the world. When talking about Red, my mother would always say he was tall, dark, and kind, which always made Red chuckle. Not a day goes by that he doesn't pop into my head. Red, after all, was the only father I had ever known.

Winter had come early that year. I remember burying Red on the first of December while it snowed. As I stood there watching perfect little snowflakes land on his glossy black coffin, I had thought to myself that Red would've been pleased it was snowing because he loved Christmas so much.

That year I had wanted to celebrate Christmas like never before. I wanted to celebrate for Red because he wasn't there to celebrate with us. I needed it to be the best so that he would know how much I missed him. I had lots of silly ideas like that when I was little.

Unfortunately, my losses culminated in a sodden spectacle, and I never did get the real tree for Red. That's why I really wanted it. It wasn't for my birthday; it was for Red. Better late than never, and better an artificial than not a tree at all. As I closed my eyes that evening, I wondered if Red would have liked a pink Christmas tree.

* * *

My lashes had just shut when this strange feeling came over me. It was similar to the uncomfortable itchiness of anticipation that I always got right before it rained. It was as if the world was holding its breath, and because of it, time was suspended, to only be woken with the first raindrop. But the rain never came. I was inside, and the longer time stood suspended, the more my dread metastasized. This suspension of time spread over my senses like a sleeping sickness, rooting me to my bed.

It was like my senses were muted and screaming at the same time. I wrenched my eyes open, my line of vision landing on the mildew-stained ceiling tiles. Trepidation streaked down my temples in beads of sweat as my eyes shifted to the right, then to the left.

In a bolt of pain, my heart jolted, my arms fighting the invisible force that kept them pinned to my sides. There he was— the man from Kip's Tree Farm. After all this time he was back, kneeling by my bedside as if he was praying at my casket.

His silver cat eyes stared down on me as I lay as motionless as a corpse. His face was so close to mine that I smelled the dry fruit of an old-fashioned Victorian Christmas tainted with decay, bringing me right back to my childhood terrors.

Not able to move, I kept my eyes glued on his strange moon-like globes as if I were a piggy bank beckoning to two shiny new dimes. I was unaware how long we stayed locked eye to eye. It felt like forever, as if seconds ticked on to years, like it would never end until my thumping heart finally gave out and I was truly a corpse.

There was a flicker of motion in his lips that drew my attention. Hope bloomed in my chest that this would all soon be over, but that hope was quickly dashed as one side of his lips twisted into a grin, then the other. At first his smile was faint, barely a smile at all, but it kept widening and widening until it became this unnatural display of teeth, and that's when his birth mark cracked. Like with a mirror, a high pitch keening accompanied the fracture in his once attractive face. Using his index finger, he picked at the crack that ran the length of his birthmark like it was a scab, chipping it away piece by piece so that I could see the hint of the bruised skin hidden underneath.

If I could have screamed, I would have. I would've screamed until my throat bled, but just as it had been when I was a little girl, my voice box had seized with the rest of my body. I was forced to watch this chipping away of skin, his eyes never leaving mine. Just as I was about to see the man underneath the handsome face, I was freed from my paralysis. Unrestrained, all I could do was scream.

Much like he had done that Christmas when the man had first visited my room, Jaxson rushed to my rescue.

"Sugar Cookie, what is it?! Are you okay?"

A warm deluge of blood trickled down my nose, fighting its way past my lips. The taste of metal made me gag. There seemed to be no end to it, and I wondered if you could die from a nosebleed. "Sorry, Jax. I got a nosebleed, and it scared me. I'm okay."

CHAPTER FOUR

Confrontation

As soon as Jaxson went to work, I headed to Kip's Tree Farm. After last night, I couldn't wait another year to cut the snake off at the head. If I had to, I would grab an axe and go 'Here's Johnny' on every freaking tree at Kip's until the man with the birthmark showed. I was going to face my fear today, 'Come Hell or high water', as my mother always said.

Jaxson had gotten so worked up last night after I screamed bloody murder that I couldn't go back to bed. His blood shot eyes haunted me, the worry in them palpable. I had really scared Jaxson, and I had promised to never scare him again. History had a strange way of repeating itself, and I'd *bet the whole 'tree' farm* that my unwanted visitor would be watching over me tonight, shedding his skin like the snake he represented. After all these years he was back, ready to stop me from moving forward. Not again—this ended today.

A light breeze whistled merrily past me as I hopped off the bus. I shoved my gloved hands in my worn burgundy peacoat and started off in the direction of Kip's.

My coat was about as festive as I got. In the store it had looked more purple than red, but in natural lighting it was definitely the color of red wine and a little too Christmassy for my taste. However, in my current mood my coat reminded me of blood, my nosebleed from last night fresh in my mind, the cause behind all that blood burning a hole in my figurative trigger finger. It was go time.

I picked up the pace, only barely enjoying the nice day despite the fact I was walking through a *Currier and Ives* Christmas card. It was sunny. The sun's rays beaming down on the snow made it look like diamonds were encrusted in the surface; how they sparkled. If snow could smile, it was smiling that day, but I couldn't.

I stopped in front of the billboard advertisement that marked my arrival at Kip's Tree Farm to catch my breath. The little hairs on the back of my neck bristled, the chill continuing down my spine, making my entire body twitch like I had just stuck my finger in an electrical socket. The giant billboard promised family fun, Santa Claus, and of course the dreaded Christmas tree. "Happy's Tree Farm," I puzzled, reading it from the advertisement as I rubbed my chin like a super villain with an idea.

Everyone called Happy's—Kip's, truncating the name of the tree farm. It was a waste of time and energy to say Kip's Tree Farm. When you said Kip's, everyone in Sweetwater knew what you were talking about. I had no idea Kip's was really named Happy's Tree Farm. Kip seemed like a strange nickname for Happy, but who was I to judge—my name's Cookie.

I shrugged it off, trudging on toward the parking lot. Despite it being nice out now, there was a blizzard warning for late this afternoon, and I didn't want to get stuck walking in it, even if I didn't have that far to go.

Christmas Eve at Kip's was the place to be when I was a kid and, judging by the full parking lot, it still was. Festive music piped through the air, accompanied with the smell of pine trees and hot cocoa. Children were unloading from vehicles like it was the first day of school and rushed toward the entrance adorned with the decorated Christmas trees that I had loved when I was a little girl.

I wasn't surprised to see the man with the birthmark wearing his iconic red plaid coat standing at the entrance, pretending to greet people. I knew why he was really there; he was waiting for me. He was there to do his job as gatekeeper—to keep me imprisoned by my fear and guilt. His eyes, as they locked onto mine, seemed less holographic during the day, but they still weren't right. Nothing about him was right. I was just glad that I was making it easy on myself, and I didn't have to cut down a billion trees to bring him out.

I marched right up to him, putting my finger in his face, the way my mother always had when I was being reprimanded. "You have no power over me!" I shouted, reciting my favorite line from Jim Henson's movie *Labyrinth*. This guy was no David Bowie in tights and no Goblin King. He was just a stupid figment of my imagination, and he was about to be decapitated, courtesy of Cookie Marlowe. Goodbye, snake.

The man's face wrinkled, his nose twitching like a bunny. "Um . . ."

"Yeah, that's right, tough guy," I said, my fists now two wrecking balls. "It's not my fault Red's dead! I didn't kill him. I didn't make him swerve and hit that guard rail!"

"Uh, um . . ." he stammered, his finger scratching at his birthmark just like he had last night.

I wasn't going to let my fear root me to the spot, not this time. "That's right, it's not my fault Red's gone and it's not my fault my mom left. That's on her, not me! So stop haunting me, you piece of shit!"

"Um . . . I, uh, think you have me confused with—"

"Stop coming into my room in the middle of the night like some fucking pervert! I'm not scared of you! This ends right now!"

I blew on him, thinking I could snuff him out like a candle on a birthday cake.

His steely eyes darted around. "Um, ma'am, please calm down. You're going to scare the children."

I knew I had to look crazy; I was talking to a hallucination, after all. This had to be worthy of the welcome wagon from Crazy Town, the hallmark of the cuckoo's nest, but I didn't care. I needed to confront him to conquer my fear and guilt and everything else I was feeling and move on right here, right now. "I'm no ma'am, I'm in my twenties asshole, and I've had enough of you!" I wound up like the iconic *Popeye the Sailor Man,* letting my fist fly like I just downed a gallon of grade-A spinach, ready to cut the proverbial snake off at the head and end this once and for all.

My fist struck his nose hard. I recoiled, cradling my hand to my chest. "Ouch."

His hand went to cover his nose where blood gushed from it. The stench of metal overpowered the pleasant aroma of cocoa and pine, settling in my stomach in an undulating knot.

"You're, you're real," I stammered, my heart traveling from my chest to my head where it muffled everything: my thoughts, my sight, my smell. "You're real!" I shouted at him.

He wiped his nose with his coat sleeve, smearing blood across his birthmark.

"With a right hook like that, I wish I weren't. I think you broke my nose." His lips twisted in a lopsided grin, and for a second I thought his face was going to crack. "If I wasn't in pain, I'd be impressed. Where'd you learn to punch like that?"

My vision blurred before I felt my legs give way. Time slowed to a crawl; everything was happening in slow motion and there was nothing I could do about it. I knew I was going down. "*All the king's horses and all the king's men couldn't put Humpty Dumpty together again,*" I muttered, my words slurring together as I pointed at his birthmark.

"Ma'am, I mean miss, are you okay?!" he asked, his strange

eyes burning with intensity.

All I could smell was blood, but the smell seemed distant—like it was being carried on the wind like a dream that leaves you as soon as your eyelids open. It was real, but it wasn't at the same time.

Before everything went black, I murmured, "You have no power over me."

CHAPTER FIVE
Strange People, Strange Places

My eyelids fluttered as my body resisted my attempt to wake up. Slowly they opened, my eyebrows pinching together in confusion. I didn't see the familiar water-stained ceiling tiles of my bedroom but a bright white smooth ceiling, yet I was on something soft that felt like a bed, and there was a pillow under my head. Dread washed over my body as I jerked my head to see the all too-familiar birthmark, but something was off. It was on the wrong side of the boy's face, and the shape of it was all wrong; and the boy, he was off too. He wasn't the same kid I had seen in the bathroom all those years ago. In place of a messy mop of brown hair was a tangle of blond curls, too light to ever be mistaken as brown. The only thing he had just right were his strange silver eyes.

It all happened so quickly, yet it felt like I was an astronaut in space defying gravity. I had opened my eyes, saw the boy, and I had screamed. I was surprised by how loud and shrill my voice had left my heaving lungs. Normally, when I saw the man, I couldn't move or scream, but I wasn't in my room and this boy wasn't *the* man. The rules had changed and the sound of my own voice buzzing like an alarm bell startled me. I closed my mouth with a snap, in awe of my own voice and the look of bewilderment on the young boy's face. He couldn't have been more than eight, there was a softness to his features, an innocence. As if it took him a moment to register I had just screamed, his eyes suddenly went wide. "Dad, she's up! You better come quick!"

I sat up, my pulse surging as the man with the birthmark stepped into the room. He had discarded his plaid coat and had on a simple navy sweater. "Glad you're up. I was getting worried about you," he told me, accompanied by a kind smile.

My eyes darted around the room like a caged animal as my brain swooned. There was a growing pit of nausea bubbling up from my stomach. My throat was dry from screaming and I swallowed down the rising need to retch. "Where am I?"

"You're at my house, specifically in the living room." My hand unconsciously squeezed the couch cushion for confirmation. "You passed out."

Cathartically, I nibbled on my bottom lip.

As if he read my mind, he asked, "You don't remember, do you?" He didn't wait for my reply. "Yep, you passed out after you punched me in the nose. I would've called an ambulance, but you regained consciousness right away. I offered to call someone to come pick you up, but you said you just wanted to wait out your dizziness. That's when I led you to the front porch to have a seat away from the crowd. When I got back to the house, I found you hadn't moved. You were still kind of out of it when I nudged you, so I helped you inside and onto the couch before you froze to death."

"How long have I been out?" I asked, avoiding the whole punching him in the nose thing.

He glanced at his watch. "Since you came inside—over an hour."

I pulled out my cell to check the time. I was hoping I hadn't missed a message from Jaxson.

"The storm must've taken the cell tower down," he informed me, pointing behind him at the glass sliding patio door that made up the back wall of the kitchen. The view would've been picturesque if I was anywhere else but where I was. It was really snowing, the snow falling in large clumps, making it a true whiteout.

Urgh, he was right, my phone was nothing more than an expensive paperweight. "When's it going to stop?"

He shrugged. "I don't know, can't get a signal on the radio either."

"My brother's going to be worried. I have to go." I went to get up and sat right back down as all of the blood rushed to my head.

"Easy," the man urged, rushing to my side. I recoiled. I didn't want him to touch me.

"Sorry," he apologized, putting his hands up in a dismissive manner. "I'm just trying to help."

"Who are you?"

"Kip."

"Kip," I repeated dubiously.

"Yeah, Kip Turner. My family owns the tree farm you visited this morning."

"Who's Happy?" I queried.

He arched an eyebrow. "Happy? Yeah, I'm happy, are you?"

"No, I'm not, I want to go home. And I meant Happy as in *Happy's* Tree Farm."

"Uh, I'm not sure what you're talking about."

The small boy scooted in between us with a plate of cookies. "Hi, I'm Thad. Now that you're up, would you like a cookie? I made them with my dad yesterday."

As luck would have it, the cookies were in the shape of Christmas trees: the red, white, and green sprinkles acting as festive ornaments. I took one to be polite. "Thank you, Thad."

"What's your name?" Kip asked me.

"Cookie."

"Yeah, despite what it may look like, it *is* a cookie," Kip said with a good-natured chuckle.

"No, my *name* is Cookie."

A wide smile bloomed on his face and my nausea grew. "Let me guess: your parents are Chocolate and Chip."

"That's not funny."

He scratched his cheek and my stomach gurgled.

"Come on, my dad joke was a little funny."

"No," I said again, as if I was saying it in front of a jury. I was put slightly at ease when his skin didn't chip away under his touch. Thinking it would help my rumbling stomach, I bit off the tip of the Christmas tree cookie. It was actually pretty good; it was shortbread, and I could taste the butter. "Kip, that's a strange name," I said matter-of-factually, shielding my face with my hand as I smashed the rest of the cookie into my mouth.

"It's actually Kipper."

"Okay, now that sounds like a dog's name."

"A golden retriever, to be exact."

My eyes narrowed. "You were named after a golden retriever, seriously?"

"Sure was. My dad's favorite dog growing up was Kipper. It's only a little strange being named after a dog and it hurts only a little bit that there were more pictures of Kipper the dog hanging up around the house as a kid than me. Speaking of my dad," he said, turning to his son. "Hey Thad, why don't you go tell Grandpa and Grandma that Cookie is up. I think they would like to meet her."

"'kay Dad," the boy chirped, running up the stairs, his footfalls echoing in the house like he was a stampeding elephant.

It dawned on me in a wave of gut-clenching dread that Kip could have been the boy I had run into when I made my hasty exit from the bathroom all those years ago. Kip could have grown up to be the spitting image of his father. That sort of thing happens all the time. It was hard to believe how much I looked like my mother. If I was right and Kip was the boy I had banged heads with, that would mean the man who approached my bathroom stall could be none other than Kip's father. Kip was real so that would make his father real, but would it make the strange visits to my room real?

Nausea slinked up my throat, threatening to breach my lips. I swallowed bile, the after-flavor souring the taste of my cookie. I knew I wouldn't be able to hold back the rush of stomach acid much longer. "Bathroom," I asked urgently, another assault of bile already filling my mouth.

"Down the hall, first door on the right."

On shaky legs I entered a festively decorated bathroom, complete with a Santa shower curtain and reindeer soap dispenser. Even the toilet was decorated with a green fur cover that went over the lid and there was a matching rug around the base of it that did a bang-up job of cushioning my knees while I spilled my guts into the toilet.

Throwing up didn't make me feel better; I wasn't that kind of sick. If anything, it drained me. It was as if I had emptied all of my energy into a fur-lined black hole.

Gazing at myself in the mirror, I scrutinized my appearance. I looked tired and disheveled, making me appear as crazy as I'm sure Kip Turner and his family must have thought I was. I had to hand it to Kip—he was cool, calm, and collected, especially given that I awoke to yell bloody murder at his son. Thad seemed resilient, but still I hoped I hadn't spooked him. The last thing I wanted to do was scare a kid like I had been scared.

I finger-combed my hair, an instant improvement that I hoped made me look more put together and less like I was ready for a straitjacket. Leaning forward, I just about pressed my nose to the glass of the mirror. It only lasted for a flash—for half of a second—but I thought I saw something strange reflect in my eyes. I stared at myself for a long time waiting for whatever it was to come back, but it didn't, and I was left in gooseflesh, only guessing at what I thought I saw in my own eyes.

Thinking that if I didn't make it back to the living room soon Kip would knock on the door, I left. I was met with a picture of Kipper—the golden retriever—hanging on the wall. I had been in such a rush to get to the bathroom, I hadn't noticed the wall full of family photos.

My eyes were drawn to a picture of Kip with a woman I assumed to be his wife. She was beautiful, with long blonde curly hair and a slim build, and looked right next to him. They were one of those perfectly-matched couples that you see in magazines and wished you had that. The photograph was improved upon by the addition of Thad, who was flashing a huge toothy smile, seemingly proud to be missing a few teeth. I found it a little odd that Kip's and Thad's birthmarks were removed with photoshop and that their silvery eyes were changed to a light brown that bordered on hazel. There was another picture next to it with the same edits, then another then another. I guessed they were insecurities for them. After all, we all have insecurities—some worse than others.

CHAPTER SIX
Roadblocks

Hearing strange voices, I poked my head around the corner to see Santa Claus and Mrs. Claus. Kip's parents evidently played the roles for the farm's Christmas attraction. They made a believable pair, particularly Kip's father. He had white hair and a long beard and was tall with a barrel belly that I was pretty sure would jiggle like a bowl full of jelly if he laughed.

"Hi there," Santa said, spotting me. "Don't be shy little girl, what's your name?"

I could feel my lips twist into an awkward smile; he was *really* in character.

"It's Cookie, Grandpa," Thad told his grandfather while he jumped in place.

"Oh, I love cookies."

"No Grandpa, *she's* Cookie."

I walked into the room, shoving my hands into my coat. "Hi Santa and Mrs. Claus."

"Cookie, this is my father, Nick, and my mother, Emma."

"Nice to meet you both."

Santa pulled me in for a hug. "She doesn't look like a cookie." He sniffed my hair. "She doesn't smell like a cookie. Are you sure you're a cookie?" he asked me, with his cheeks as rosy as every picture of Santa Claus I had ever seen.

"Nick, please," his wife said. "You're smothering the poor girl."

"Sorry to disappoint you, Santa—Nick—but I am *a* Cookie. Cookie Marlowe."

"Not a disappointment. You're as sweet as a cookie, of that I'm sure."

"Too bad she's not going to be around for you to find out," Kip said. He turned to me and whispered, "He just ate, but I don't trust him when he rubs his stomach like that."

I laughed out loud; I couldn't help myself. In an attempt to be polite, I smothered my laugh with my hand.

"Well," Kip said, addressing his family. "We better head out before the snow gets worse."

"Do you have to leave?" Thad asked me with big eyes. "We're going to make a gingerbread house."

"Your dad's right, I should get going. The snow is really coming down. Thank you for the cookie. It was very good."

He ran to the kitchen and grabbed another and handed it to me. "For the road, in case you get hungry."

I could feel my smile reach my eyes. "Thanks Thad, I appreciate that."

* * *

I followed Kip into the kitchen, where we left via the sliding door. We stepped outside into the driving snow. It was a true whiteout, the likes of which I had never seen. The wind whipped around me, nipping at my nose, and sending a chill like a PICC line straight up my spine. I had been cold since I woke up on the Turners' couch, but now the cold seemed superhuman. It was like Father Winter himself was visiting Sweetwater for Christmas. My lungs burned with every inhale and my heart ached as if the cold was slowly killing it, like it killed everything; this slow death reaching my

34

extremities; where they stiffened.

Fluttering rapidly, my eyelids tried to shake off the onslaught of icy snow. The crystalline snowflakes clung to my thick lashes, weighing them down, as if the snow wanted me to close my eyes and fall asleep. Kip took me by the hand and led me off the porch, his touch warm. "This way, Cookie. The truck's parked on the side of the house."

He opened the passenger-side door and helped me into his truck. Once I was situated, he went around to the other side to start the engine and cranked on the heat. "One minute, let me get some of the snow off," he said.

Sitting in the truck shivering, I wrapped my arms around my midsection and watched Kip push the snow off the roof of his Dodge Ram with a push broom before taking an icepick to the windshield. The way the ice shattered off the glass in irregular sheets of condensed snowflakes brought me back to my bedroom—to Kip scraping away at his own skin.

I closed my eyes for a moment to regroup, opening them to see Kip smiling at me, his eyes bright—beaming. "Almost done!" he shouted. A shudder of bitter cold wracked my body. My imagination was clearly on steroids. I had gotten his smile just right. More than that, I had every little detail exactly spot on: from his coat, his hair, his eyes, his birthmark, even his perfectly maintained five-o'clock shadow. It was eerily accurate—too accurate. There was something just not right about him.

I gave Kip the thumbs-up before shoving my gloved fingers into the vents on the dashboard. Cool air was piping through them but compared to the temperature outside, I might as well have been on a tropical island.

Kip got into his truck, taking a moment to dust the snow off his clothes before it melted. "Geez, this is one heck of a storm."

"You can say that again."

The windshield wipers came alive. "What's that?" I asked, pointing at a clearing in the backyard. I hadn't noticed it while plodding along in the blizzard, but there was a large patch of land that didn't have snow-dipped evergreens.

"A lake."

"Wow, that must be great this time a year to ice skate on! Do you guys ever ice skate?"

My mind was transported back in time to when Red had taken the family ice skating. It was a happy memory I still clung to. I could never forget how he held my hand the entire time to make sure I wouldn't fall. Red may not have been in my life for long, but it didn't matter—he was the one my heart longed for. Red would always be my father.

"Not so much anymore," Kip said, shifting into reverse. "So, what direction? Where do you live?"

"Willow Commons."

"Perfect, that's not too far away. I'll take 7th Avenue. I think that's our best bet."

"No," I said louder than I meant to.

He let his foot idle on the brake.

"Take Dorset instead," I insisted.

"I was just thinking there would be less chances of oncoming traffic if we take 7th Ave."

"Please," I urged as tears blurred my vision. "Take Dorset."

"Okay, Dorset it is," he said as the car crawled in reverse.

The road was completely hidden under snow, and I knew Kip was driving off memory. Even with four-wheel drive, I was worried we could get stuck.

We drove on at tortoise speed in silence for a long while before I spoke up. "Sorry about yelling at you this morning. I thought you were someone else." I owed it to Kip to apologize. He had done nothing wrong, and he was now seeing to it that I got home. He could have left me outside to freeze to death, but instead he brought me into his home even after I had assaulted him. "And, uh, sorry about your nose."

He pinched the tip of it. "Good news: you didn't break it." Glancing at me and grinning, he added, "Or that could be bad news, if that was your intention."

"I was trying to knock your head off," I admitted. It sounded funnier in my head than how I delivered it, but he smiled anyway.

"Well, I think a couple more practice shots and you will be ready to take on the world. Crime fighting might just be in your future, just make sure you get the right guy next time."

I grinned at that.

"But, uh, Cookie, I think after the blizzard dies down you should file a restraining order on whoever you thought I was. If you need someone to go with you, I can go. It sounded like you got yourself into a pretty bad situation with my doppelgänger."

I nodded. I needed more than a restraining order, I needed to kill him, kill my fear. I felt like I needed to do that to truly move on. I had to bury the past so I could enjoy the future. It would be a lot easier if I could make sense of the past and why my mind placed Kip in my bedroom. The only thing I knew for sure was that Red was dead, and my mom split.

"Funny enough," Kip said, glancing at me out of the corner of his eye. "I think I've met you before. I didn't mean to stare at you this morning. You were just so familiar to me."

My heart skipped a beat. "Really?"

"Yeah, it kind of freaked me out when you charged toward me thinking you knew me. I've been racking my brain trying to figure out where I know you from. I'm usually good with faces."

Anxiously, I rubbed my hands on the tops of my thighs. "When I was a kid, my brother took me to your family's tree farm. I ran into a little boy outside the bathroom and almost knocked him over. We bumped heads—"

His voice came alive. "That's it! I remember! You had a huge fit and were freaking out, crying and screaming."

I felt my lips flatten to a straight line.

Seeing my reaction, he chuckled. "I mean, you were upset. I thought I had really hurt you. Let me tell you, I had a lump on my forehead for about a week after that. Sorry."

"It was me who ran into you."

"I know," he conceded. "But the way you were crying, it felt like it was my fault, so sorry all the same."

"Was there a man with you?"

"Uh . . . I think I was by myself." His eyes cut to me, "Why?"

"Your father, was he always a big man?"

"Yep, he likes to say he's big boned."

"So, when you were little, he was husky?" I enquired, not wanting to call his father fat.

"Yep, always husky. Why do you ask?"

"You don't look like him."

"Nope. I've always been told I look like my mother, but my father and I definitely share a similar sense of humor."

That was true enough. He did look like his mother. I imagined one day Kip would take up the mantel of Santa Claus for Kip's Tree Farm, or was it Happy's Tree Farm? But Kip would definitely need to pad his stomach. His eyes though, he seemed to have gotten them from both his parents.

"I thought I saw this man with you that day we collided. He looked how you look now, but there's no way it could have been your father."

"Yeah, not my dad; but you saw this place this morning. It's always mobbed. I'm sure it's more than possible there could have been someone there that day that looked similar to how I look now."

"He even had your coat on," I said, touching it to make sure it was real.

"I wouldn't worry about it. This is just a run-of-the-mill generic coat. I got it at Home Depot last year. I'm sure lots of men have similar ones."

"Maybe," I supposed, rubbing my arms. The heat was coming out full blast, but I was still cold.

"Maybe?" he repeated in a leading way, turning the heat on as high as it would go.

"I don't think you get it. The man I saw, I think he was you, like, actually you. I know I'm about to sound crazy, but do you think it's possible that I glimpsed the future? That I got it all wrong and you weren't there to scare me? I don't know, maybe we were supposed to meet," I sighed, putting my whole body into it. "Okay . . . that sounds even crazier than making you up in my head to find out you really exist."

He flashed me a kind smile. "Who's to say what's possible and what's not? It's Christmas time, anything's possible. My late wife, God rest her soul, always said, 'Christmas makes its own magic' and I believe that. I wouldn't want to ever scare you, and I like the idea that we were supposed to meet."

"You do?" I asked, as all of the heat in my body rushed to my cheeks. It just dawned on me that I hadn't met Kip's wife, and now I knew why.

"Yeah, I do. It makes that lump I had to walk around with worth something."

I could feel my flush deepen. I was being stupid, reading into things. What was wrong with me anyway? An hour ago I was terrified of Kip and now I was—I don't know—wanting him to like me? I was more of a headcase than I thought.

Frustration coated my eyes with fresh tears. I couldn't wait for this day to be over. I hated Christmas more than ever. Taking the cookie from Thad out of my coat pocket, I ate it in two T-rex bites, wishing I could do that to the whole damn holiday.

Kip kept his eyes on the road as he spoke. "You're very interesting, Cookie Marlowe, and now that I know you're the one who gave me that knot on my forehead way back when, I think you should make it up to me. Seriously, I had to walk around with *Pinocchio's* nose growing out of my forehead for a week. How about after Christmas, you let me take you out to dinner? How's that sound for an act of atonement on your part? I'll even shake things up and wear a different coat, unless you're particularly fond of plaid. Your call: Calvin Klein black dress coat or can-you-believe-it I work on a farm red-plaid-classic."

Hope warmed my chest, thawing out the icy feeling that had clung to my heart since I woke up to find myself on Kip's couch. I couldn't help myself, and in truth, I didn't want to. "Dinner sounds nice, and let's go with the black coat. I'm trying to move forward."

Kip slammed on the emergency brake. The car lurched forward. I held my breath, my stomach in my throat. The truck skidded to a stop a few inches from a fallen tree that laid across the road. It was covered in snow and blended in with the stark backdrop. I didn't even see it until after Kip went for the break.

"Wow, that was close," he gasped, catching his breath as if he had just finished a marathon.

I placed my hand over my heaving chest, hoping to steady my heart rate. "Shit. Do you think you can move it?"

He glanced at me, then at the huge tree in the road. I knew it was a stupid question, but I had to ask.

"Um, I hate to disappoint you, Cookie, but I really am a farm hand, and not the *Hulk*. The red plaid isn't just for show, it's practical. But not to worry, I will turn the truck around and try 7th Avenue."

"Let's just go back to your house. I'll wait out the storm."

"You sure? We're already out here."

"Yeah, I'm sure," I said as I twiddled my thumbs.

With a lot of effort, Kip was able to turn his truck around and soon we were heading back in the direction we came from.

"So, what's up with 7th Avenue?"

I didn't answer.

"Well?" he prodded.

"My stepfather died on 7th Avenue on his way to pick me up from school. I never drive on it."

"I understand," he told me.

"No, you don't," I hissed, my emotions getting the best of me. "It's my fault. If I didn't stay after school for Girl Scouts, he would still be alive. I knew he hadn't been feeling well. He had hurt himself at work, but I still went to my Girl Scout meeting. Because of my selfishness I destroyed my family, Christmas, and myself."

He chanced a glance at me, keeping both hands on the steering wheel. "I do understand. My wife, Ellen, she died last year. Today is the anniversary of her death, in fact. I've been trying to keep that moment out of my head all day. You've been a nice distraction," he said with a sad smile.

"Last Christmas Eve, I took Thad shopping after the farm closed for the day. It's a little tradition we have. You know, go out with the last-minute shoppers, soak up all of the excitement. We don't go crazy, I just take Thad to the dollar store, and he picks out silly gifts for everyone. The lake you noticed, well, when we were out shopping my wife went onto the ice. She was a professional figure skater. No one moved on the ice like her. She had grown up in Florida. Having spent almost all of her time skating in inside rinks, she loved skating outside. She always said it was natural, nature at its purest, that it just felt different. Last winter was a warm winter; still, I was positive the lake had frozen over. It's not a deep lake. It's man-made. I made a mistake. I told her it was safe to skate on, but it wasn't. While Thad and I were out shopping, she hit a soft spot in the ice. By the time we got home, it was too late."

My chest tightened, a horrible feeling consuming me. "I'm so sorry."

"Me too. It would be easy to blame myself. It was me, after all, that gave her the green light to go skating."

Kip kept his steely eyes on the road as he drove, the snow and ice crunching under the tires like broken glass. "I've replayed that day in my head so many times. There were so many little things that could have saved Ellen. If only I had asked her to go shopping with us, or to wait to skate until we got home. But I can't change the past." He glanced at me. "None of us can. Trust me when I say I understand. It would be easy for me to quit. To let the guilt gnaw at me until there was nothing left, but I have Thad. I can't just shut myself off from the world. I can't let him think because his mother died that I gave up, or that he should. Or that he should hate skating now or Christmas, or, God forbid, me."

I wiped a tear before it could spill over. "When my stepfather died, it changed everything. That Christmas I had wanted it to be the best, but I let my guilt eat me up, turning it into fear—fear of the holidays, fear of enjoying myself, fear of being close."

"Your brother, what's his name?"

"Jaxson."

"You're not alone Cookie, you have Jaxson. And you have to be strong for him; he lost your stepfather too."

"Red was his father."

"All the more reason for you to be strong for him. So, tell you what, let's start by taking 7th Avenue and getting you home. You should be with your brother, celebrating Christmas Eve and Red."

He did understand. "Thank you, Kip."

* * *

As Kip approached 7th Avenue, he pumped the breaks,

letting his truck coast to a stop. He drummed on the steering wheel with the palms of his hands. "Well, that sucks."

I swallowed my tears, not able to speak. The bridge was out. The very bridge that Red had hit black ice on. I felt like I took a step forward, to only be yanked back an entire football field by my hair.

"I know my family is not Jaxson, but we would love to celebrate Christmas Eve with you, Cookie. Who knows, maybe you were meant to spend Christmas with us this year and the universe is just putting you where you need to be."

He smiled and his strange silver eyes shimmered. Kip was great and so was his family, but I just couldn't shake the feeling that something wasn't right about all of this.

CHAPTER SEVEN
Different in the Dark

I awoke in the middle of the night, the nagging feeling of being watched wrenching me from my sleep. My eyes scrutinized the room while I lay perfectly still. I knew very well where I was and was expecting to see Kip kneeling by my bedside. Not the real him of course, who I had gotten to know pretty well after spending the evening with him and his family, but the Kip Turner that I had made into some sort of Hell spawn *Humpty Dumpty.*

My body tensed into a protective ball in anticipation of something God awful. My pulse was steady, kept that way by sheer will. The last thing I wanted to do was make a scene and scare Thad. I didn't know how meeting the real Kip and sleeping in his guest room would affect the concoction I had willed into existence.

After a thorough back and forth of the room that made it feel like my eyes were spinning around in my head, I sat up and the search began again. The muscles in my back and shoulders relaxed with a methodical exhale. Smiling, I internally congratulated myself. It was over. All of it was over. I had confronted my fear today when I punched Kip in the nose, and now it was over. There was no boogie man hovering over me while I slept; I was alone.

My relief was short-lived. There was this growing sense of dread that seemed to wrap around me like a cocoon, constricting as if to prepare me for my metamorphosis. It prickled the little hairs on my arms in a reverse domino effect. I attempted to shake it off, running my hands gently down my arms. I told myself this growing trepidation was just because I was snowed in at a strange place, with people I just met. It was Christmas Eve—I should be at home in my bed.

In my bedroom the lights from the parking lot bled in through the slotted blinds, but at Kip's house a thick curtain covered the sole window in the room, allowing only a pinprick of light to cut across the gray carpet in a slash of yellow.

In the daylight, the guest room had looked clean and tidy, and just perfect. It was the sort of bedroom I wished I always had: spacious, bright, and decorated with French accents. I felt like I was spending the night at one of those posh châteaux I'd seen on TV. I wasn't sure who had decorated it, Kip's mother or his late wife, but they had done a beautiful job. When Kip had opened the door to show me where I would be sleeping, I teared up. The Turners' guest room was a far cry from my dorm room and my bedroom, that oddly enough looked and felt a lot like a dorm.

I had crawled into the guest room bed happy, feeling like I was on vacation, or what it must be like to be on vacation. Jaxson never had a lot of money. How could he, when he had to support me from such a young age? I never missed vacations and those sorts of things. You can't miss what you never had, but being snowed in at the Turners' ended up not being so bad.

We had made it back to the tree farm just in time, before the snow and ice doubled down. Even if a tree wasn't lying across Dorset and the 7th Avenue bridge wasn't out, making it to Jaxson's apartment was impossible. There would be no going out short of the *Heat Miser* orchestrating a volcanic eruption and there were no volcanos in New Jersey, not at least any I knew about. I just hoped Jaxson wasn't worried about me.

SECOND CHRISTMAS

I felt a little guilty I ended up having such a great night, while Jaxson was most likely sitting at home or stuck at work wondering if I was okay. I wished Jaxson could have been with us tonight. This evening with the Turners reminded me of family time while Red was still alive: the laughs, the teasing, the warm feeling that comes with being loved. The Turners weren't selfish, they let me share in that warmth and as I dunked my cookies in milk, I felt like I belonged. It was an amazing night of playing games and constructing gingerbread houses and watching *It's a Wonderful Life* two times, back-to-back, until finally Thad fell asleep, and Kip carried his son to his bedroom.

Today had been an eye-opener for me. I think Kip was right and I was supposed to spend Christmas Eve with his family. I went from being creeped out by Kip's face—hating it—to enjoying it, all in one day. Red was dead, but I wasn't. If Kip and his son could live on after their loss, so could I. I owed Kip—a lot. He saved Christmas for me this year, and for every year after.

Despite recovering my Christmas spirit, I was finding it increasingly difficult to hold on to. As my eyes adjusted to the dim room, it dawned on me how different everything looked in the dark. I felt like I was seeing the room for the first time—really seeing it. I saw how tired the paint was on the walls, how it shed from the plaster like an overripe banana peel, leaving the plaster dappled in grim moldy splats. The furniture that had transported me to the French countryside was now shabbier than it was chic. *Everything* seemed so different in the dark—different and cold.

My dread spread under my skin, covering me in gooseflesh, my metamorphosis now complete. I was a Christmas turkey—more to the point, a goose. I always hated the feeling of those little impromptu pimples on my skin. I tried to rub them out, but it had the opposite effect. Goosebumps pricked down my arms and up my legs, the sensation converging in the small of my back. It made me feel like something was trapped under my skin and trying to claw its way out of me, little pimple by little pimple.

I knew I wasn't stuffed with bugs fighting for their escape from my meat suit or anything as macabre as that. I wasn't the *Oogie Boogie Man* from *The Nightmare Before Christmas*, I was Cookie Marlowe, and I was just cold. I never really did warm up. It felt like the cold was a part of some sickness I was inflicted with, and cold and dread go hand in hand. The Christmas spirit was about feeling warm and loved amidst the bitter chill of winter, literally and figuratively. I just needed another blanket, and things would stay on track.

My head jerked toward the closed guest room door. I thought I heard something, but it was hard to hear anything over my chattering teeth. It was as if they chewed their way into my brain and were now gnashing in my ears.

I got this silly idea in my head. It came to me in a flash and warmed me with a smile of pure childish delight. I saw Kip in his father's Santa suit, as it hung on his thin frame, crouching under the tree with gifts for his son.

With that pleasant image snugly secured in my mind's eye, my feet hit the carpeting. There was no warmth to be gained from it—I might as well have put my feet on stone. The carpet was stiff against my wool socks as I tiptoed to the door. I took care to turn the knob ever so slowly so as not to ruin the moment—the moment every little kid waits for on December 24th—the arrival of Santa.

I slipped into the living room as if I was a phantom, not making a sound, my ethereal presence unknown. Not that there was anyone to be known by; there was no one there. I was alone.

In the dark the living room took on the same worn-out vein as the guest room. Everything appeared old and disheveled, as if the night had infected everything with its gloom.

The gun cabinet stood tall and dark like a coffin in between the living room windows where curtains hung from them like discarded lace wedding dresses. Wraith-like, I approached the windows that looked out upon the expansive tree farm, taking in the stillness that seemed to have swallowed the house. Under the glow of the moon's half smile I could see the tops of the snow-covered evergreens. In response to the golden beam, the trees glistened as if they shared the moon's fickle mood. The Christmas trees stood still, tall and menacing. These soldiers armored with snow and sleet guarded the house. Or were they stopping us from leaving—stopping me from leaving? Again, I thought everything looked different in the dark.

Tentatively, I let my fingertips brush the iron radiator under the window. It was ice-cold to the touch, and I realized what I most likely heard was the heat kicking off, or more likely the sound was the electric going out as the Christmas tree in the corner was unlit. With the cell tower down, it stood to reason the electricity would soon follow. I considered us lucky that we got through the night as we did with the way the snow was coming down.

My eyes kept gravitating toward the Christmas tree. Earlier that evening the tree had been a spectacle of rainbow-colored lights, the bubble lights sparkling like a witch's brew while the crochet snowflakes embellished with teeny tiny silver sequins twinkled like stars. The tree was a lifetime collection of handmade trinkets and novelty ornaments, making it all-Turner, and I loved it.

In the absence of the family and light, the tree looked scared, its once proud branches cowering to the dark. Approaching the tree, I noticed that the vibrant green needles of the most beautiful Christmas tree I had ever seen were brown and dead. Under my light touch, the pine needles fell to the floor like dirty fingernail clippings. "What happened to you?" I whispered to the tree, as if I expected it to answer me.

The tree didn't answer, but someone did. "I drowned," the

unknown voice told me.

My head snapped toward the unfamiliar tenor. Standing in front of the glass sliding door in the kitchen was a slender, beautiful vision of a woman. I was frightened and in awe all at the same time. My heart pitter-pattered in my chest, my eyes glued to the woman, unable to look away. She radiated a warm glow, as if she had fallen from the moon and moon dust covered every inch of her. Her eyes were closed, her dark lashes arching in two smiles. Her wavy blonde hair clung to her head as it made its way down her back like a ripple in water. At first, I thought she was wearing a white dress, but it wasn't a dress, it was a long coat.

That's when I heard it. The distinct sound of a *drip-drop.* The sound only liquid can make. It was akin to the tune my blood pandered to during one of my epic nosebleeds. *Drip-drop. Drip-drop.* Instinctively, my hand went to my nose to catch the blood, but there was none. The familiar dribble was coming from the woman. She was soaking wet, and I realized if her hair was dry, it would have been curly like Thad's. Water beaded down her long tendrils, pooling at her feet where I noticed she was wearing ice skates.

Who she was hit me like a ton of bricks. "You're Ellen," I muttered, the majority of my voice locked in a spasm in my dry throat.

"I drowned," she repeated again, as if she was in a trance, and I wondered if she was sleepwalking. A shiver slinked up my spine, making every inch of me tremble like my teeth. She wasn't sleepwalking. She was dead.

I spoke in a soft voice, just above a whisper. "I know. Kip told me. I'm sorry that you drowned."

"I'm sorry too," she replied with the same indifferent cadence.

"What do you have to be sorry for?"

"I'm sorry that you drowned," she said, repeating my words

back to me.

An electric spike of pins and needles shot up the side of my jaw all the way to my temple, leaving my teeth on edge. Before I could close my mouth, Ellen was on the other side of the glass sliding door. I raced toward her, no longer careful on my feet as I was compelled beyond my will to follow. I think I would have followed her all the way outside if I hadn't stepped in water. The cold liquid instantly penetrated my thin socks and snapped me out of whatever spell I had fallen under. I caught my breath, confusion washing over me like an ice bath as my hand went to my damp socks. They were soaking wet. There was water all over the floor—lake water.

Light-headedness attacked me from all directions, and I thought I was going to faint.

"Cookie," Kip said, turning on the lights. "Are you alright?"

I spun on my heels to see Kip with his hands full of presents, my legs wobbling under me for a moment before I stood tall. "Hi," I rasped breathlessly.

With the lights on I felt instantaneously better. It really seemed like the dark atmosphere had been suffocating me. It was a silly thought, but the truth often is. I could breathe now. I hadn't realized I had been holding my breath until the force of my overdue exhale almost threatened to knock me off my feet. Everything was back to normal. With the light came the dazzling Christmas tree with branches upon branches of lush pine needles with their multicolored glow that made me feel warm and fuzzy inside. I hoped that meant the heat would be steaming out of the radiators in no time.

"Sorry, I didn't mean to scare you," Kip told me before placing the gifts in his hands under the tree. "I know my dad dresses up as Santa, but I'm the real Saint Nick around here and it was time for me to come down the chimney."

I laughed it off. "By now you know I scare pretty easily. I'm not a tough cookie."

He smiled and his strange eyes twinkled like the lights on the Christmas tree. Patting his nose, he said, "I don't know about that; you're pretty tough, and so was that dad joke. Can I call a pun a joke—let alone a dad joke—if you're not a dad?"

"I'll admit it, *tough cookie* was on dad joke status," I said, with what I knew had to be an awkward smile. Smoothing out my sweater with both hands, I found a stray string at the hem that I wrapped around my finger before pulling it off. "I, um, was thirsty," I quickly added, realizing Kip was probably wondering why I was walking around his house in the dark like a burglar. I was grateful he didn't show up a few minutes earlier and catch me by the Christmas tree. That would have painted one heck of an unsavory image: crazy girl passes out at tree farm then robs nice family of their Christmas gifts in the middle of the night.

"What's your poison, Cookie: water, iced tea, chocolate milk, or eggnog? I'm going with eggnog with a shot of rum."

"That sounds great," I said, hoping the adult beverage would help me get back to bed. It usually did. Back at college, one beer and I slept like a baby. I imagined rum should work like a charm.

The piece of loose string I had wound around my finger dropped to the floor and I noticed the puddle of water was no longer there. I felt my socks. My feet were cold, very cold, but were they damp? I didn't think so, but there was no way I had imagined Kip's dead wife. She had been there.

I felt my blood turn to ice in my veins as my eyes fell on the deep scratches leading to the sliding back door. It was as if someone had walked on the hardwood wearing ice skates. I spoke excitedly, nervous energy finding its way into my voice box. "Kip what's that?!"

He popped his head out of the refrigerator. "What's what?"

I pointed.

"Um, scratches."

"From what?"

He shrugged before opening a top cabinet and pulling out a bottle of Bacardi Rum. "Who knows, Thad's a rough kid." He chuckled to himself as he poured the rum into two mugs of eggnog. "I was a rough kid too. My mother is nuts about keeping the floor polished to preserve the life of the floor. I hope she doesn't notice those scratches until after Christmas."

"You grew up here?"

"My grandfather started the tree farm. My father's lived here his whole life and so have I for the most part, Thad too."

"Who put in the lake?"

"My grandfather. His dream was for Kip's Farm to be this Christmas attraction that people from towns near and far would flock to for ice skating, buying their Christmas trees, and visit with Santa."

"Mission accomplished. Your grandfather must be Happy," I chirped, taking my mug from Kip and heading back to the glass slider to look out toward the lake.

"Yeah."

Happy's Tree Farm became Kip's Tree Farm; it was a family legacy. There was something nice about that. Taking a sip from my mug, I tried to hide my aversion to rum. It wasn't for me. I think Kip overdid it. I couldn't even taste the eggnog. He must have been a pirate in another life.

Yep—pirate: Kip added more rum to his mug and leaned against the counter. "Every year more and more people come here to just walk around, which is fine, but it just seems like no one is buying live trees these days. Nothing kills a tree farm like artificial trees. Can you believe I saw a pink Christmas tree at Walmart this year? Seriously, what will they think of next? Whatever happened to tradition?"

A hot flush rushed to my cheeks, and I hoped Kip thought it was his dousing of rum that had caused it. "Walmart has nothing on your trees," I muttered, glancing back at the twinkling Christmas tree in the corner, and past it to the snow-clad sentinels on the other side of the window.

"You got that right," Kip agreed full-heartedly.

Guilt over my pink Christmas tree purchase directed my eyes back to the barren landscape of the snow-ladened lake. "What's that?" I asked, feeling like I was on repeat. The moonlight faintly illuminated thin tracks in the snow that disappeared into the dark. Those hadn't been there a moment ago. I was sure of it.

Kip joined me by my side.

"You see it," I said, putting my finger to the glass door.

His eyebrows stitched together. "Uh, I think so . . . Um, so why am I looking at this?"

I swallowed my answer. No good would come of telling Kip I thought I saw his dead wife and that I thought she was skating around the property. I had to reel it in, big time. "I was just wondering what kind of animal made those tracks," I lied. "I was thinking raccoons were out their having snowball fights with squirrels or something."

"Raccoons have been known to instigate snowball fights around these parts," he laughed. "I love your imagination."

I stared into my mug, the tips of my ears burning.

"You don't like it, do you?"

"Hmm . . ." I muttered, meeting his gaze.

"The eggnog."

"It's a little strong."

"No problem," he said, taking my mug from me and dumping it into his.

"You're not worried about germs?"

"I'm not worried about *your* germs."

Another wave of heat slapped my cheeks, and I felt warm all over. I was no longer cold, but hot. Kip went to the fridge, refreshing my glass and skipping the alcohol altogether.

He met me back by the slider. Taking the mug from him, I took a sip. "Much better."

Kip clanked his mug with mine. "Merry Christmas, Cookie."

I was forced to look at him to return the sentiment, my cheeks scorching. I don't know how I had ever felt cold. I felt like I could've walked outside and been perfectly fine, the snow melting to my will. "Merry Christmas, Kip."

"Do you feel it?" he asked, his eyes narrowing until they were a line of silver on his handsome face.

"Feel what?"

A streak of pink highlighted the bridge of his nose. "Um, I'm not sure how to put it without coming off wacky, but there's something between us. I know we just met, but it feels like I've known you for years. Please tell me you feel the same and that I'm not destined for the loonie bin."

I had known Kip, in a strange way, most of my life. His face had haunted me in every sense of the word. It was so strange how something can scare you and excite you at the same time. That amalgamation shouldn't exist, but it did with Kip. Part of me still wanted to run from him, and at moments punch him in his birthmark to see if his face would crumble like a broken ornament, but the other part of me—the part of me that was winning out—wanted *all* of him. This must be how a moth feels—enticed to the flame—drawn to the heat of the moment, drawn to the danger of it all.

"You have strange eyes," I blurted out, feeling a little bit like *Little Red Riding Hood*. I didn't mean to, it was just that I felt so much like a helpless moth and his eyes were beckoning me closer.

He laughed out loud. "I've been told I have nice eyes a couple of times, but I've never gotten strange."

I flashed him a sheepish smile, my eyes still locked with his.

"I'm sure you get it all the time," Kip said, dropping his voice to a whisper. "Your eyes are so unique. They're beautiful."

Having light blue eyes, I got that quite a bit. "Thanks. I do, but it's still nice to hear you say it."

He brushed a loose strand of my hair off my cheek. His touch was so cold, I instinctively recoiled. "Sorry, your hand's cold."

"Apologies. The heat must be having a hard time keeping up with this wonky weather."

He leaned in and planted a chaste kiss on my lips. I pulled away from him again. The many nights that I had awoken to find the man who looked like Kip crouching by my bed, he had merely watched me and chipped away at his face. He had never kissed me, but as Kip's lips touched mine, a feeling of déjà vu swept over me, and I knew that the man had in fact kissed me before.

A deep crimson blush bloomed across Kip's face, his birthmark taking on a liquid shine.

"No, it's okay," I promised. "You just took me by surprise. Remember, I spook easily."

"Then it would be okay if I kissed you again?"

Before I could respond, his lips connected with mine and he delivered a real kiss. The coldness of his chaste peck was long gone; in its place was warmth, as if he had swallowed the sun.

I closed my eyes. The taste of alcohol on his breath mingled with the sweet savor of fruit that had haunted my nights as a child. It was like I was tasting apricots and raisins, oranges and apples. I didn't mind the rum now—in truth, I wanted more. I wanted the whole damn bottle and all of him, every little inch of him.

Our lips sliding together, the familiar smell and taste of fruit hit a crescendo. The déjà vu moment strengthened, blurring Kip with the imaginary man that had visited me in my bedroom. I forced my eyes open. Kip's eyes were closed, but hers weren't. Over Kip's shoulder I saw Ellen, her eyes gleaming at me like two silver moons.

I pushed Kip back with my free hand, breaking his hold on my lips.

"Sorry," I gasped, the perfect moment lost. "I didn't mean to shove you. It's not you, I just don't want to ruin the moment."

"I understand. I have a hard time stopping once I get going, and I don't want to ruin anything with you, Cookie."

"Good night," I said, placing my mug in the sink. My eyes darted to the lake just in time to see Ellen disappear into the endless night, but I knew she wasn't truly gone.

"Good night, Cookie."

With my heart in turmoil, I left Kip standing in the kitchen. It was better for me to go. Three was a crowd. If Kip could have chosen between me or his wife, I knew he wouldn't pick me. Yeah, she was dead, but she haunted his thoughts, and evidently him. Kip was spoken for. In many ways I felt like I owed Ellen—she had saved me from running blindly into a flame that would've burned me alive.

As I waved a final goodnight to Kip before shutting the guest room door, a growing part of me wished Ellen would've just stayed dead and let me burn.

CHAPTER EIGHT
Christmas Morning

A murmur of indistinct voices serenaded me through the guest room door, and I knew the Turners were up. I rolled out of bed, having slept well after I tired myself out thinking about Ellen and Kip and Kip and me. Doing the best I could, I finger-combed my hair in the mirror that hung above a French provincial dresser, pulling my long hair back into a high ponytail.

I opened the door to the smell of Christmas breakfast.

"You're up," Thad cheered, jumping off the couch. "Can I open my gifts now?"

"When your dad gets back," Nick told his grandson from the kitchen table where he was dressed in his Santa suit, smoking a pipe like he was the real deal.

"Good morning and Merry Christmas, dear," Emma said to me with a bright smile. "How did you sleep?"

"Merry Christmas. Uh, great, thank you. Um, where's Kip?" I asked, joining Thad in anticipation.

Before Emma could answer, Kip came through the front door.

"Dad!" Thad shouted, running to his father and hugging him, seemingly not caring that he was covered with snow. "Cookie's up, can I open my presents now?"

"After breakfast," Emma scolded.

"But Grandpa said when my dad gets back."

"Yes, but now breakfast is done."

"Dad," Thad whined.

"One now. The rest after breakfast."

He ran to the tree.

Kip took off his red plaid coat and hung it on the coat hanger by the door. "Bad news, Cookie," he said to me, his eyes on his son as he searched under the Christmas tree for the perfect gift. "Even if I could dig out the truck, the roads aren't clear."

Hot air escaped my breath in a huff.

"Not to worry. I'll get you home to spend Christmas with your brother. I'm up for playing horse—who's up for a sleigh ride?"

"Me!" Thad shouted. Having found the present he wanted, he tore it open. It was an action figure of some superhero I wasn't familiar with, but Thad seemed really pleased, his silvern eyes sparkling like his father's.

"Can I open another one?"

"After breakfast," Kip told him in a kind voice.

"But I'm not hungry."

"After breakfast."

"What about the sleigh ride?"

"After breakfast, if that's okay with you, Cookie?"

I could feel Emma's glare burrowing into the back of my skull. "Of course," I said.

"Well then," Emma chirped. "Everyone sit down, and I'll get breakfast on the table."

I felt as excited as Thad rummaging under the Christmas tree as Emma placed muffins and sweet buns and bacon and eggs and pan fries and French toast on the table. There was fruit salad and bagels and toast and donuts, orange juice and apple juice, coffee, tea and punch. The Turners knew how to do Christmas breakfast.

"Before we eat, we have to say grace," Nick reminded everyone. He had been very quiet this morning. He was a far cry from his larger-than-life persona of yesterday. It was true he was still dressed as Santa, but today's Santa was very somber, especially for

Christmas morning.

"Go ahead, Thad," Kip urged. "Why don't you read the prayer you wrote at Sunday school?"

Thad raced up to his room, leaving his action figure on the table. Thad's footfalls sounded like Santa had landed on the roof with his eight tiny reindeer as he took the staircase. In no time at all, he was back in the kitchen unrolling a paper scroll.

"Thank you God for a world so sweet.
Thank you God for the food we are about to eat.
Thank you God for my mom with angel wings.
Thank you God for everything.
Amen."

"Amen," I said in unison with the Turner family.

Prayer over, I went for a muffin, my mind on Ellen from last night, her ghostly form vanishing from thought as the smell of freshly baked blueberries conquered all, making my mouth water. They smelled just like the ones my mom would make for Red around the holidays. Before I could take a bite of my muffin, my attention was brought to Nick. At first, I thought he sneezed, and I was about to say God bless you, but it wasn't a sneeze at all—he was crying.

The sleeve of his Santa suit was cupped to his mouth, stifling a wheezy sob. As if he pushed the remainder of his feelings back down his throat, he lowered his hands, his eyes wet with tears. "This—all of us happy—sitting around the table for breakfast, reminds me of the good old days, doesn't it Kip?"

"Yeah, Dad," Kip agreed, his face blotted in pink, no doubt from seeing his father crying. At first it was just a few vagrant tears that rolled over his lower lashes, but they were falling steadily now, his rosy cheeks streaked with salty nostalgia.

"Grandpa, are you okay?" Thad asked, his silver eyes widening.

"No son, I'm not. Turners have always stuck together. Family meant something when I was a boy."

"Nick," Emma said in the stern voice used by women around the world when dealing with their husband's caprices, a voice cultivated over years of marriage.

"You listen woman, you all listen," he said, pointing his finger at his wife before it made its rounds to the rest of us, including me, eventually settling on Kip. "Kip, this is all my fault."

"Umm . . ."

Getting up from his seat, Nick made his way into the living room.

"Uh Dad, It's okay. Just sit down and enjoy breakfast."

"This last year I've seen how sad you've been. You and Thad and Emma. Seeing you happy the last two days made me realize how miserable I made you. It was more than she ever did."

"Dad," Kip pleaded. "Please, sit down and have some breakfast. Mom worked hard on it. Don't let it get cold."

Kip's mom whispered to me, "I'm sorry, he must have visited the bottle this morning. He does that from time to time since Ellen passed."

"She was going to leave you, you know? She was done with couple's therapy."

Kip's eyes darted to me. "Dad, this is not the time. Now please, sit down and eat breakfast."

Asking him to sit only seemed to fuel Nick's emotions. Loud howling sobs broke through his quivering lips, his face as red as his Santa suit. "She was going to leave you and make us sell the farm, and she was going to give it to him."

"Dad," Kip said, his eyes cutting to me again. "Not now. We have a guest and it's Christmas."

"I was home when it happened. I was home and I . . ."

"Thad, sing a song," Kip ordered, clamping his hands over his son's ears. Thad did what he was told and started singing *Santa Claus is Coming to Town*.

"I heard her when she yelled for help—screamed for it—and I ignored her. I sat right there," Nick said, pointing to the kitchen chair he had just gotten up from. "I sat there, and I watched through the back slider as she drowned."

Emma gasped, covering her mouth. Kip, on the other hand, was silent, his face frozen in time, but the color had drained from it. His skin looked porcelain, as if he was a doll, and I feared he would crack open, just like I had seen his face do so many times by my bedside.

Kip kept his hands clamped over his son's ears as Thad continued on with his Christmas carol, starting over in ignorant bliss as he moved the arms of his action figure up and down as if it was conducting a grand orchestra.

"I thought she was getting her just deserts, getting what she deserved for two-timing you and your boy, and that it was best she just drowned and was forgotten about. But it didn't make a lick of difference. Ellen died for nothing; the farm's still going to him. He bought it Kip, from right under our noses. He paid all the back taxes. Happy owns the farm now. It's all over."

"Happy's Tree Farm," I muttered.

Kip's eyes acknowledged me before he focused his attention back on his father. "We will work it out, Dad. Please, just have a seat and enjoy Christmas breakfast with your family."

"Family . . ." Nick repeated as if he was contemplating what the word meant. Finding the meaning, his conviction grew, letting it be known in his voice. "That's right, Kip—family. This is our land. My father made Kip's Farm what it is, and I will be damned if another family lives in our house and lives off our land, sweat, and tears. The farm was for Thad and his family, and his son's family after that. The farm was *our* legacy!"

"Dad," Kip pleaded, some color returning to his face. "Please, that's enough. I don't want to discuss this in front of Thad and Cookie."

"You're right about that, son. It has to be enough. I'm at the end of my rope, we all are. I'm just glad in the end, you were happy." His finger circuited the kitchen table again. "That we were all happy. This will always be our house, our land. It belongs to us, and I will make sure no one ever wants to step foot on Kip's Tree Farm again."

Nick went to the gun cabinet and pulled out a shotgun. I didn't know much about guns, but I knew what a shotgun looked like. Without another word, he aimed it at the table and yanked back the barrel. It sounded like a bomb went off between my ears. Emma was knocked to the ground before I registered what was happening. Her eyes were wide open, the shock having just reached them as the shogun slug hit her heart. Bright red blood flowered over her white sweater, the smell of metal mixing with blueberry and bacon made my stomach churn.

There was a click. My head snapped toward the sound. Nick took aim at Thad. With a clothesline to his son's chest, Kip knocked Thad and the chair he was sitting on to the ground. They had just hit the hardwood as another bomb sounded in my head. I was on my hands and knees now. There was a ringing in my ears that made my entire body tremble.

Kip clutched my hand. "Get Thad out of the house. Go across the lake. It's the fastest way to a neighbor. The lake's frozen. Trust me."

The sound of Nick's heavy boot scuffing across the pine floor echoed in the room, drowning out the ringing in my ears that had already silenced the uncontrollable beating of my heart. I could feel my eyes expanding in their sockets as I glimpsed his tree trunk legs through the lace tablecloth. Santa was coming for us.

"Go now," Kip pleaded, his silver globes webbing over in red as if spiders lived in his eyes. "Please, keep Thad safe."

Grabbing Thad's hand, I yanked him off the floor as I scrambled to my feet. My boots felt like they had lead soles, but still I dashed for the sliding back door, dragging Thad along with me.

The sound of dishes breaking and silverware hitting the floor as the kitchen table was turned over rebounded in my ears as I slid the back door open. It was a strange cacophony of sounds. The silverware being thrashed about sounded pretty, like the tinkling of a wind chime in a summer breeze. It was in distinct contrast to the high-pitched whine of the broken dishes, as if good versus evil were having it out in the Turners' kitchen.

I pushed Thad outside, turning around just in time to see a slug rip through Kip's cheek. It happened in slow motion, in snail time. I felt like I could see time, see the slow hand of the clock work its worst as the shot unforgivingly tore through flesh and splattered Kip's brain on the kitchen cabinets. I saw everything: Nick's hand on the trigger, the shotgun slug whizzing through the air, the look on Kip's face. His eyes were on me before they closed forever, his body falling to the floor in a bloody heap.

Time returned to me in a horrible wave, bringing with it sound: the bang of the gun going off, the thud of the slug's impact, the squelching of brain matter as it hit a hard surface. My legs wobbled as bile rose in my throat, burning it. Kip was gone before I could even muster up a scream, before I could even say goodbye.

The cold sting of the wind rushing in from the open door, and Thad's small hand in mine, spurred me back to reason. I had to keep Kip's son safe. He had asked me to. It was the last thing he said to me, or anyone, and I was going to do it.

I swallowed the acid in my mouth, pushing further outside. Everything as far as I could see was white. More snow had fallen last night. It was so beautiful, and yet so unbelievably daunting. It looked like the colorless world in front of me stretched on forever. I couldn't see *the light at the end of the 'lake'*. The closest neighbor was far—very far.

I looked at Thad, whose small face was contorted in worry. He was in his pajamas and Spider-Man slippers; there was no way he was making it across the lake like that. I crouched down. "Hurry, get on my back. He's right behind us."

"But my Dad—"

"Your dad's coming. Now come on Thad, jump on my back," I urged, trying not to scare him.

He did as he was told, and I gripped onto his legs to anchor him. My adrenaline was pumping through my veins, giving me superhuman strength. I could no longer feel the cold. The sting of it, that had borne down upon me since I woke up on Kip's couch, was gone. I was all energy and impulses now. It was as if Thad weighed nothing.

I stepped off the back porch, my feet sinking through a layer of ice into soft snow. I was buried in it up to my kneecaps. I tried to remain calm as I lifted my leg to take another step. Nick would have just as much trouble with the snow as me, and I was younger and was in better shape. I could do this. I could get across the lake and save Thad. At the same time I thought this, I saw Kip in my mind, saw the look in his silver eyes as they dimmed to brown at the moment his brain turned to mush, and my resolve buckled with my legs.

I heard the sliding door open behind us, but I didn't dare look back. The grating noise of the door on the track and the promise of what that meant was all of the motivation I needed. Nick didn't have to catch us. He just had to have a decent aim, which he had already proven to have. Hiking Thad up on my back, I went as fast as I could toward the lake, even though I knew we were sitting ducks out in the open without the cover of the Christmas trees that stared at us, unblinking. Not so much as one twinkle winked our way as the sun hid behind thick gray clouds.

"Cookie! Over here!"

It was Jaxson. Relief permeated through every inch of my fiber at hearing my brother's voice. "Jax!" I shouted as I did my best to run to him, where he was hiding behind a Douglas fir.

I rushed into Jaxson's embrace, not bothering to put Thad down. As his arms wrapped around me, I felt safe. I knew it was only temporary, but I soaked in the moment, burying my cheek against his chest, not knowing and not caring how he got there.

"Cookie, where's my dad?" Thad sniffed. "I want my dad."

I lowered Thad, wrapping him in a hug to keep him warm. "He's coming." I looked to my brother. "Jax, where's your truck? We have to get out of here now!"

Jaxson's dark eyes glazed over. "I have tried everything to save you, Cookie, but it always ends the same."

I felt my face wrinkle. "What are you talking about? Save

me?”

"You can't stop Nick. You've tried. I've tried. For the last five years on Christmas, you've come here—to this very spot—and it has always ended the same. You can't save the Turners."

The cold's icy grip penetrated my hand where I held onto Thad, the sting kissing up my arm. "What are you saying?"

"Cookie, oh Sugar Cookie, you couldn't save the Turners and you couldn't save yourself. Five years ago, you died. You spent Christmas with the Turners that year, and it was your last."

The cold had made it to the nape of my neck, threatening to invade my brain. "That's not possible . . ." I muttered, a brain fog falling over me.

He seized both of my hands, breaking my grip on Thad. He squeezed them, and I felt it. I felt it like I had never felt anything before. That was proof he had no idea what he was talking about. I was there and he was there, and Thad was there, and Kip was dead. Shot in the face, right through his birthmark.

I felt like a lightning bolt had struck my spinal column, the surge zapping my brain and moving aside the curtain that had kept me in the dark. Kip's birthmark—the birthmark that was missing in all of the family portraits on the wall. The birthmark that Kip's doppelgänger kept scratching at. The birthmark that had cracked under his smile, revealing a hole in his face.

I glanced at Thad, my eyes narrowing in on his birthmark that was so similar to his father's. I knew then it was an omen. Thad was going to die the same way as his father, with a shot to the face.

"How do I die?" I asked Jaxson in a whisper, trying to shield Thad from as much of our conversation as possible.

"You drowned in the lake."

My body crumpled in on itself as I leaned against my brother for support. I knew he was telling the truth. I felt it deep inside of me, in my marrow, where the cold had originated from, cold as unforgiving as the water that took my life.

Ellen had told me the same thing last night, but I hadn't wanted to see what was right in front of me. I saw her because I was like her. Her eyes were a strange silver because Death had coated them with its derision, just like Kip's eyes and Thad's and all of the Turners, myself included. I had caught a glimpse of the silver in my own eyes. It was as if there were two coins hiding behind my blue irises, ready to be given to the ferryman of lore as payment for rowing me to the afterlife; but I never made it, none of us did. We were all still here at Kip's farm.

"I don't understand," I panted, trying to make sense out of it all.

"I don't either," he admitted. "All I know is that for the last five years, you've shown up the day before Christmas Eve, dead set on getting a Christmas Tree. You just show up, having no idea you died. One way or another you come to Kip's Farm. I've tried to stop it, but can't. I've taken Nick's gun, but it doesn't matter, he finds another one. The result is always the same."

"We can still save Thad," I urged, taking Thad's hand again.

Jaxson's eyes moved to a half-lidded position. "He's already gone, Sugar Cookie."

Tears stung the back of my throat, where they clawed the lining mercilessly. "No, he's not. I wouldn't be here if there was no hope. Why else am I here, then? If everything you're telling me is true, why come back here if I can't change anything?"

"I don't know why you keep coming back, Sugar. I really have tried to help you. I've tried it all. Believe me, I've tried it all. I've even accompanied you to the Turners', and every time you die. I love you more than anything. God, I love you, Sugar Cookie. You're the reason I live. I came here today so you wouldn't be alone in the end. So you would know, no matter what, I will never leave you alone."

"You're not going to help me?" I asked, my voice cracking as my tears broke free from their prison.

"Sugar, there's nothing I can do."

I tasted the blood in my mouth before I realized I had suffered another nosebleed. Before I could wipe my face, Jaxson did. I could see it, the crimson smear on his white glove. It was there.

It was more proof that we were all there. Jaxson had to be wrong. He must have made a mistake. I wasn't dead. How could I be? I could taste the metallic bite of blood on my lips, feel my heart beat savagely in my chest, feel Thad's small, cold hand in mine as he shook. Something strange was afoot, but I wasn't dead—not yet.

Nick's voice boomed in the still morning. "Thaddeus, come here boy, I want to show you something!"

Nick was too loud, as if he wasn't stalking toward us but was in my head with his shotgun aimed dead-centre at my brain. If it weren't for my eyes telling my mind he was the bright red blight a ways off in the snow, I think I would've collapsed from a self-induced bullet to the cranium.

I could see Nick, the red spot coming closer with every passing second, and I could see my footprints. Nick would know where we were, there was no hiding. My footprints were the perfect breadcrumb trail; it was like inviting a killer to a buffet.

"Come on, Thad. Your dad is waiting for you to open your presents," Nick said joyfully, as if he had resumed his role of Santa Claus.

I placed my finger over my mouth and shook my head. It was true our footprints marked the spot, but Nick would have no way of knowing how deep into the tree farm we had gotten.

"You're going to love what I got you. It's a paintball gun. You saw it, didn't you Thad? In the kitchen? Grandma was just playing. Now come give it a try, it's so much fun. You can shoot me."

Thad's eyes widened, and I could see the wheels turn in them. He believed his grandfather, thought it was all for play. Nick's betrayal sent a spasm through my jaw as I clenched my teeth, the moment the shotgun slug ripped through Kip playing over like a horror movie in my brain. I went to tighten my grip on Thad, but it was too late, he had pulled free of my hand and was rushing toward his grandfather.

"No, Thad!" I screamed, chasing after him. I grabbed him by his shoulder, yanking him to me as an upsurge of warm blood sprayed my face. I fell back with Thad, the snow cushioning our fall, the sound of the gunshot still ringing in my ears.

I was on my knees, Thad's body pillowed on the snow. The taste of his blood was in my mouth now, searing my throat with reality. This was really happening. "Oh God, no!" I begged, my hands clasping his small, angelic face surrounded by blond curls that hung as lifeless as him. His silver eyes had dulled to a vacant brown. The wound on his face was small, going through the birthmark on his cheek where a scarlet pool filled the hollow under his cheek bone. The back of his head had already painted the snow around us crimson in gore. In his outstretched hand was his Christmas present from his father. He was gone. Thad and his father were both gone.

I looked to Nick, not able to say out loud the question my heart screamed at him—*why*—why are you doing this? Thad and Kip and Emma were more important than the farm. Home is where the family is, not the other way around, and his family was all dead.

Nick evaluated me with blank eyes; there was no remorse there—there was nothing—they were merely twin silver daggers, and their sights were set on me.

I forced myself off my knees. Nick was close now, closing the distance between us and blocking my route back to Jaxson, where he remained hidden behind a Christmas tree. I had only one choice—the lake.

I moved quickly over the frozen lake, as if by compulsion. I could see the trees on the other side of it and knew if I could just reach the tree line, I would be safe.

My head jerked like an owl's at the sound of Nick's gun going off, and I knew the loud pop of the blast would haunt me forever. I stopped running, placing my hands on my knees while I caught my breath.

Nick raised his shotgun, taking aim. There was no way he could hit me, I was more than halfway across the lake and Nick was still ashore. My relief was momentary, lasting only the fleeting second it took for Nick's face to twist into a sneer. Cold seeped in from my toes, spider-walking up my legs to my heart. He wasn't aiming at me; he was aiming for the lake. He was going to shatter the ice floor like a mirror.

Jaxson stepped out from his hiding place. He was so close and yet so far away. I wanted to run to him and have him make everything okay, but I knew—deep down inside, I knew—that he was right and this was the end for me. Denial could only get me so far. I was going to drown, like I had for the last four years. It was like Jaxson said: I couldn't save the Turners, and I couldn't save myself.

I squeezed my hands together in prayer. "Please God, don't let it end like this."

I could feel my warm tears on my face, feel them worm down my cheeks where they mixed with Thad's blood and mine. This was the end, or was it? There was a chance, a good chance, I would come back next Christmas.

Jaxson flashed me a bittersweet smile, and I knew it was my send off. I knew what was coming next. The sound of the ice cracking was a prelude to my icy death.

"I love you, Jax. I'm sorry," I said in a whisper, my voice, like my hands, tied up in a yarn ball with all of my regrets.

The bang of Nick's shotgun rang out again, the sound bringing with it a burning, stabbing cold that pierced my heart. I wasn't sure if I was breathing or not, or if I ever was. I wasn't sure if I was alive or dead; maybe I was some New Age version of the living dead—living dead girl. All I knew was cold—I could feel it, and I feared it.

My eyes gravitated to Thad where he lay in the snow, his bright red blood a macabre snow angel. The remorse and pity I felt for him and his father and for myself consumed me. I felt so alone, so helpless. Christmas had come and it was the worst Christmas ever, apparently like the year before, and the year before that. Kip had given me back Christmas and I had failed him. I looked up to the cloudy sky, murmuring another prayer. "Please God, let this all not be real."

SECOND CHRISTMAS

Sparkles fell from the sky in the form of snowflakes. One landed on the middle of my forehead, and I knew then I was marked like some sacrificial lamb. God wasn't going to save me. I was going to have to save myself.

I had promised to never scare Jaxson again; yet I couldn't think of anything scarier than him having to watch his little sister drown. There was no room left for secrets. I called to Jaxson on the shore, "Next Christmas tell me everything as soon as I come back. Everything! How the Turners die, how I die. None of this makes sense. Nick loved his family. Something dark is attached to the Turners. I think I saw it when I was a little girl in the bathroom when you took me to Kip's Farm."

As if to silence me, Nick unloaded his gun. Shots showered around me as a light breeze rattled the ornaments in the trees. It sounded pretty, like the trees had made their own Christmas carol just for me. But like all things beautiful, they break down and decay, and this merry tune would ultimately serve as my funeral dirge.

The time was now. The high-pitched keening of the ice breaking under my feet cried out in a hideous lament that made my entire body tremble. I could hear it crack, hear the ice splinter off as the water unforgivingly rushed under the ice, pushing into the fault lines and widening them.

As if the Earth had opened its mouth, I fell into the lake. The cold was unlike anything I had ever experienced. The chill that had burned my heart could not have prepared me for the fiery Hell of the ice water. It felt like I was trapped in a Jello mold again, the water seemingly thick and heavy as I fought to gain purchase on the ice and pull myself to safety.

Something tugged on my foot. In the murk of the water blonde locks of hair were visible, they undulated like the many arms of an octopus. Then I saw her silver eyes—her cold, dead eyes. I shook my head, clawing at the ice above me. I didn't want to die like this—with her. I wanted to die with Kip, with Thad. I wanted to be with them. I deserve to be with them, not in the cold and dark with the woman who had broken Kip's heart. I realized as Ellen pulled me deeper into the gloom of the lake that I wanted to die in Kip's arms, but that would take a Christmas miracle; and as Ellen found out when she met her end, Christmas doesn't make its own magic. *Misery loves company* should have been the slogan painted on the sign for Happy's Tree Farm.

CHAPTER NINE
Next Christmas

"You want me to go with you?" Jaxson asked as his truck idled in the parking lot of Happy's Tree Farm.

"No, I have to do this on my own." Instinctively, my hand felt for the folded newspaper article in my coat pocket. Kip would have to believe everything I said once I showed him what the local paper called 'The Christmas Tree Farm Tragedy'. After all, it was what Jaxson had shown me to make me believe. It was all there: the date, a picture of the Turners, and a picture of me.

Reading an article that spelled out your own death is . . . well, like something out of a nightmare, like a children's flip book made in Hell. But I wasn't dreaming, I was alive, in my own way I was a living, breathing person. Maybe I was living my own personal Hell, doomed to ride out the worst day of the year for eternity. I already hated Christmas, what more did God or the Devil want from me? I suffered, according to the article in the Sweetwater Herald, I really suffered along with the entire Turner Family, Nick included, as after he had finished brutally murdering his family and me, he turned his gun on himself.

I glanced over the many beautifully decorated trees, knowing it was now or never. There was no getting around this—I had to face Kip Turner, the man who had haunted my dreams. He had been at the center of my night terrors, hovering over me like some pervy guardian angel, and I was sure he was the reason for my premature gray hairs. Still, I was there to save him and his family.

Stranger than a ghost that could polish off half of a breakfast pizza, was seeing Kip's face in the article. I had stared at it for who knows how long. It was a nudge from Jaxson that had broken my hold on his paper eyes. I knew his face so well, it was practically seared into my eyelids. In the article, Kip didn't have the strange birthmark that in the gloom of my bedroom would crack under the burden of his creepy smile, revealing something dark and nasty underneath. I knew why that was—Jaxson had made that point quite clear as he held up two fingers like a gun and said, "Bang." Kip's birthmark was the aftermath of his death—an echo, a stain—and somehow, I had seen it when he was a little boy that day I ran into him. I had known he was going to die, without understanding it.

It was the same thing with Red. I had seen the bruises around his neck for a week before he suffered the car accident that had claimed his life. I had thought he had hurt himself at work, but that wasn't the case. I *had* seen things, but didn't know what they meant. Knowing that I could have saved Red and Kip and his family ate at me from the inside out, turning my stomach in knots until my breakfast threatened to make a reappearance. How could I be dead and hurt this much? I had failed to save Red and the Turners, but for some reason I was given yet another chance to help Kip and his family. I didn't think you could save someone who was already dead, but I was there, and he was there, and there had to be a reason for that. All my mushed-up brain could think to do was to spare his family from being slaughtered again.

Shutting the door to the truck, I gave Jaxson a reassuring nod and the thumbs-up. Turning from him, I pulled my coat closed. For being dead, I was sure cold.

I approached the entrance to the tree farm, my boots sinking into the snow to a festive soundtrack. I wasn't close enough yet to make out which Christmas song was playing, but I could see the ornaments glistening where they hung from thick green sprigs, smell the fresh sent of pine and dried fruits, and I could see the red plaid coat that I knew belonged to Kip.

SECOND CHRISTMAS

I took a deep breath, letting the cold air sit in my lungs until it hurt. Fists clenched at my sides, I approached Kip Turner. I had waited long enough, giving him as much ignorant bliss as I could afford. Tomorrow was Christmas; this had to be done now. His back was to me; but I would know him anywhere. I thought, as my feet padded in the snow, that I would know him if I were blind. I couldn't help but feel like I was trapped in a snow globe. The familiar tune of *Santa Claus is Coming to Town* tap danced on my temples, awakening old memories, old Christmases, old feelings.

The recollection of chattering ornaments as the wind joined the chorus whirled around me in a brain fog. I knew I had been there before, and it had nothing to do with Jaxson telling me. I had stood right where I was standing. It was so familiar: my outfit, the way the sun made the freshly fallen snow sparkle, the way Kip stood at the entrance to the tree farm—the key to all of this.

I pushed myself in front of Kip. "I need to talk to you," I huffed out in a desperate gush of hot air, my breath piping out of my mouth like a steam locomotive.

A smile bloomed on his face and the birthmark that had always been there stretched and screwed under the burden of his expression. I kept my eyes on it, rather than being sucked into his silver globes. It was a reminder of why I was there—to save him—to stop a shotgun slug from giving him a lobotomy he could never come back from. It was the promise of death, and all I wanted to do was grab his face and kiss him better.

A flush burned in my cheeks at my thoughts. I had feared Kip almost my entire life. To have other feelings for him beyond that surprised me and confused me at the same time. I felt like the snow globe I was trapped in had just suffered a blizzard, my brain numb from the aftershock.

"Sure," Kip chirped, as if he didn't have a worry in the world. "I'll help in any way."

I knew he was dead and that I was dead, but everything felt so real: the cold nipping at my nose and chin, the smell of dried fruit wafting off of him like he rubbed an orange under his armpits as a holistic deodorant.

"In private," I added, twisting my hands together in front of me in a pretzel.

Pensively, he raised an eyebrow before lowering it. He looked like he thought I was going to hit him over the head with a club and kidnap him. Seriously, would that be so bad? I figured that would be most men's idea of a very merry Christmas; it wasn't like I was a Christmas troll or anything.

Jax had told me that he thought I had feelings for Kip, though I never confirmed it. How could I have? I was too busy getting murdered by a wannabe Santa Claus.

I could never know what I felt for Kip that first Christmas that claimed our lives, but standing in front of him as I was now, I knew there was undeniably something between us. I wondered if he felt it, though the evaluating eyebrow would lend itself to a *ho* no.

I yanked Kip's arm, dragging him deeper into the tree farm. When he planted his feet, I was forced to stop. I was no match for his strength. This wasn't where I wanted to do this, but he left me no choice. It would be easier to make my point if we were standing in front of the billboard welcoming us to Happy's Tree Farm, but things don't always go your way, and I had to work with what I was given before I lost Kip completely and he stormed off to his death.

"What color eyes do I have?" I quizzed, my hand still gripping his forearm.

His face twisted as if I had just asked him a trick question. "Umm . . . gray, uh, no—more like silver. They're very pretty," he said as a blush colored his complexion.

"No. My eyes are blue."

He raised a finger in protest, but I didn't let him get a word out. "It's proof," I blurted, and the crease between his eyebrows became more noticeable. "Listen, Kip, you don't know me, but I know you."

"Um, okay, I'm listening," he said, trying to nonchalantly free his arm from my hold, but I wouldn't let him go. I dug my nails into his coat, ready to go skin deep if I had to. He had to hear what

I had to say. I didn't care if he thought I was really trying to kidnap him, or that I was crazy—he had to hear this.

"Long story short, I met you when we were kids, right here at your family's tree farm. I ran out of the bathroom, and I bumped heads with you."

A smile spread across his face, pulling on his birthmark. I shook my head at myself. I had to stop thinking of it like that, it wasn't a birthmark.

"No way," Kip told me, his smile growing until it spread ear to ear. "I remember that. Sorry for the clash of heads. Glad to see that I didn't cause you any long-term head trauma. So, what's your name? I should probably buy you a hot cocoa or something for the knot I'm sure you had on your head. I know I had one."

"Cookie Marlowe."

His grin shifted to the side. "Your parents Chocolate and Chip?"

I could feel my mouth turn down into an ugly scowl. It wasn't his dad joke, per say. Okay, that was part of it, but he was just so freaking happy, and I was about to do more than rain on his Christmas plans. Merry Christmas Kip, your face is about to get blown off.

I let go of my death grip on his arm to fish out the newspaper article from my coat pocket. "I don't know how to say it, so just read this."

He took the article from me and unfolded it. He had only glanced at it for a moment before he folded it back up and pushed it into my open hand. "That's not funny."

"You have to read it, all of it," I insisted, claws out ready to latch onto his arm again.

"Listen, Cookie, this is a family place. So just leave and have a merry Christmas."

"You don't understand, I die too. I was with you and your family." I grasped his hand. He tried to pull away from me, but I held tight. "Please, let me show you something. Then I'll leave and you will never have to see me again."

He sighed deeply, his shoulders slouching. "Show me what?"

"You have to follow me."

Again, he tried to pull his hand from mine, and this time he succeeded. "No offense, but I'm not following you anywhere."

"It's not far. I just want you to come look at the billboard for your farm. The one at the entrance in front of the parking lot. I pointed onward. "Not far at all."

"Please tell me you didn't vandalize the sign right before Christmas?!" Kip rushed past me; I followed. He stopped in front of the billboard, running his gloved fingers through his dark hair as he evaluated it. "Why did you do that?" he asked, glancing my way. "Why go through all of the trouble to change the name on the billboard?"

"I didn't change it, Kip. He changed it when he bought your family's tree farm six years ago. Happy, that is. The same man your wife was having an affair with."

He narrowed his eyes until they were slivers of silver moons. "What are you talking about and how did you know about Ellen and Happy?"

"It's all in the article. Check the date." I handed him back the newspaper clipping. This time he read it—slowly—and I watched the color drain from his face until he was as pale as the snow that painted the landscape in the Christmas spirit.

"I don't understand," he finally said, handing me back the article with shaky hands.

I shoved it into my coat pocket, not taking the time to fold it. "Trust me, I know. I feel the same way as you. But the truth is, we are already dead. We've been this way for a while. You saw the date, right? Every Christmas you and your entire family relive their deaths." I could tell by the way his eyebrows pinched together he was mulling it over. "Think about all those families you were greeting moments ago. Did any one of them acknowledge you or say merry Christmas back?"

He glanced in the direction we had come from, before his

steely eyes found mine. "Just you," he said in a near-whisper, his anxiety making its way into his trembling voice. "I don't get it. I mean, I can't be dead and neither can you. I felt your hand take mine." He bent down, taking off his glove and picking up a handful of snow. "I feel this."

"I don't understand the rhyme or reason, but know that I am in the same boat as you—I can feel." I placed my hand over the snow that still sat in his palm, the moisture penetrating my glove. My raw emotions clawed up my throat and I did everything in my power to swallow them down, forcing them into the bowels of my churning stomach. If I could feel his hand and the snow, that meant I would feel every moment of what I knew was to come, unless I stopped it.

"I have to admit, this all feels oddly familiar, doesn't it?" he asked while he nibbled on the inside of his cheek. "When you came up to me, I thought to myself: Now where do I know this girl from? But I don't get it, why do you remember all of this, and I don't? If what that article says is true, I think I'd remember dying—dead or alive. And you said this happens every year. Why then don't I have any recollection of it?"

I smashed our hands together, not caring about the snow. "It's true, Kip. It's all true. And I didn't remember either. I'm still not sure if that's a blessing or a curse. My brother, he knows what's going on, he filled me in."

"Wait, I thought people couldn't see us?"

My jaw snapped shut. They couldn't, but yet Jaxson could.

"Well, if what the article says is true and your brother can confirm it, then all I have to do is take my father's shotgun and the disaster is averted." He squeezed my hand; the snow trapped between our palms had completely melted via our body warmth. "To be honest, it's hard to believe my father—near impossible—would do that. In fact, I can't believe it. He's been playing freaking Santa Claus for the last twenty years. If it wasn't for the strange feeling I get when I'm with you, I wouldn't even be entertaining this, but I have to think about my son and if it's true, what that means for us."

"I know, I get it. I read the article. People were shocked, but taking your father's gun doesn't work. We've tried that. For the last six years Jax has let different scenarios play out."

"Okay, what haven't we tried then? Maybe we should call your brother. And what happens to us afterwards? Is this the last day I have with my son?" He glanced back toward the entrance to the tree farm. "I, I should go check on him."

"This is new—us knowing we are dead. What happens next, I have no idea."

He was back to nibbling on the inside of his cheek. "Okay, so what do we do with that knowledge? We're dead and somehow we can still be killed because for some reason we can still feel," he hashed out, thinking out loud as his eyes fixated on our hands. "And we can't pick up and run because we're already dead."

"I have an idea—well, it was Jaxson's idea really. It's scary and crazy but we haven't tried it."

"I'm listening."

"The lake."

"What about it?"

"I always drown in the lake, trying to get across it for help. This year we have to make it across. Your father cracks the surface by shooting at the ice. We just have to get across it before Christmas breakfast. That's when he goes killer Santa. Enjoy your night with your family and tomorrow meet me at the lake at dawn. Make sure your son and mother are with you. This, whatever this is, is tied to Christmas, so we have to do it on Christmas. Jaxson thinks if we can cross the lake, Heaven will be waiting for us on the other side. There's no way of knowing for sure, but it's the best shot we have at stopping the cycle." I winced at my wording.

"Okay," he said with a nod. "I can do that."

Just then a small boy with blond ringlets ran up to Kip. "Dad, I've been looking all over for you!" Kip released my hand, and I instantly felt colder. He knelt to hug his son before picking him up and hoisting him onto his hip. "Thad, this is Cookie."

My eyes landed on the little boy's birthmark. I knew who he was as soon as his mop of curls came into view. I had seen his picture online amongst the other articles highlighting 'The Christmas Tree Farm Tragedy'.

"Hi, Thad."

He smiled at me in a way only an innocent child can smile. I felt this instant connection to Kip's son. It was as if I had known him for years, and in a strange way I had. I had known them both. I could feel my smile wane under the burden of the future as my eyes glazed over. This was all going to happen again.

CHAPTER TEN

The Lake

My eyelashes fluttered as I struggled to open my eyes. They felt glued together, but as the hold was weakening—it had to—I could sense that someone was in my room. I did my best to control my breathing, knowing what I would see when my lashes pulled apart. It was him—Kip—or at least some perversion of him.

Sweat collected in my hairline as I strained to open my eyes. This had never happened before. I had always been able to open them. Something had changed. I would have pried them open, even clawed at my own lids if I could have, but I was tied down, held by invisible hands.

There was something worse in not seeing. It was like being trapped in the dark where every monster in every child's closet was lying in wait. I really needed to see him, needed to confirm he was there at my bedside so I could prove to myself he wasn't the real Kip. The real Kip was a nice man and a good father, this stranger in my waking dream was just that—a stranger—and I needed to make him go away. Kill him or it, or whatever he was.

Rapidly, my chest heaved up and down out of my control as if my heart was trapped inside an expanding hot air balloon, to only be deflated the next second. I gave up, releasing all of the tension in my body that had nowhere to go. It didn't matter that I couldn't see him, I could smell him.

The smell of fruit tickled my nose; accompanying it was the hint of rot that crept farther and farther into my nostrils, activating my gag reflex. He was moving nearer—I could feel him, sense him as he inched his way closer to my face.

An ice-cold touch grazed my cheek. It was so cold it burned, and I wondered if he was cutting my face with his nail. His white-hot touch traveled down the angle of my cheekbone to my nose with precision.

I became aware that my nose was bleeding, the taste of its metal tang just breaching my lips. My eyes opened as if by magic and there he was, with his raised finger glistening in the dim light. It was painted red with my blood.

I changed my mind. I didn't want to see him, but now my eyes were glued open. Kip was there as he had been when I was a child, exactly how he looked just earlier that day at the tree farm, down to the same winter coat.

Kip put his finger to his lips, letting it linger there before he slid it into his mouth. He smiled down at me with his silver eyes that were as cold and cutting as sheet metal. I tried to scream for Jaxson, but I couldn't. I couldn't do anything. I was completely helpless. I had never felt so small and so scared.

His smile seemed crueler tonight—more twisted—as the commissures of his lips pinched upward, cracking his birthmark down the middle. The ballooning of my chest as my heart beat faster accelerated the effects of my nosebleed. It was in the back of my throat now, choking me. I tried to swallow but my throat was paralyzed.

Kip leaned over, pressing his mouth to mine, his tongue darting between my lips. I could feel it as his tongue spooned my blood into his mouth. I felt like I couldn't breathe. *I couldn't breathe.* I was choking. Oh God, I was really choking. He was suffocating me. I was drowning in my own blood.

My vision blurred, turning his face and his silvern globes into smears as my lips burned with an icy cold that traveled down my chin, down my chest, toward my heart. The smears of color were turning black at the edges now, like dark hands—shadow hands—acting to blindfold me. I tried to breathe, but all I did was suck my own blood and his tongue deeper into my throat.

Just when I thought it was lights out for me permanently, he was gone. I sat up ramrod straight, coughing up blood as I greedily gasped for air, not caring that I was ruining my *Garfield* comforter that I had since I was a little girl. Frantically, I wiped at my lips, the flavor of rotten fruit having made an unholy matrimony with the metallic taste in my mouth.

My eyes darted to my alarm clock; it was Christmas morning.

* * *

I walked to Kip's Tree Farm while it was still dark out. Shadows as thick as the snow painted Christmas morning in gloom. To add to my foreboding, my feet hit the snow in a deafening crunch. The temperature had plummeted last night, and a layer of ice had formed over the snow. Every footfall had its own echo. The doomsday clock was counting down the minutes.

Jaxson and I had agreed last night, before we went to bed, that this was something I had to do without him. If my plan to get across the lake failed, that meant I would drown. Although he said he had always been there for me in my last moments, I could see in his eyes how much it had cost him. I didn't want him to go through that again. Previous Christmases I hadn't known I died, but now that I knew what was waiting from me at Kip's, the least I could do was spare my brother seeing me drown again. Not that I planned on failing.

SECOND CHRISTMAS

Entering the empty parking lot of Kip's, the sun peeked over the trees in the distance, casting a golden haze over the treetops that made it look like the stars were still out and twinkling. It was beautiful in a chilling kind of way, as if the heavens guided my path.

I walked through the tree farm to get to the lake, not wanting to alert Nick that I was there. For this to work, we had to sneak across the lake without him following us with his *boomstick*. As I passed a wild turkey nestled soundly under a Christmas tree, I felt as if I was stuck in that snow globe again, breathing in the same stale air. It was too early for the songbirds to be making merry and there was no wind. It was as if the entire world was sleeping besides me. I prayed Kip took me seriously and would be waiting for me at the lake.

I wasn't sure if crossing the lake would actually save us, and Kip's question of what happens afterward plagued me. I had no clue what would happen if we escaped the Turner Christmas massacre. It didn't really matter at this point. Whatever was waiting for us on the other side of the lake was better than the alternative, it just had to be.

I felt frozen to the core before I made it to the back of the property, a feeling that intensified when I saw the lake stretched out before me in icy brilliance. Jack Frost had painted the ice with delicate crystals that made it look like the lake had been decorated for Christmas, or perhaps it was for me—symbolic flowers on my soon-to-be resting place. The thought sent a slow shiver down my spine, as if someone had taken their time to run an ice cube down my back, making sure to hit each vertebra.

There was a dark spot on the horizon; I could just make out the red of a coat. It was Kip. He was alone. Why was he alone? I jogged in his direction, stopping a few feet from him to catch my breath. "Where's Thad and your mother?"

"I just wanted to see you before I got them. I wasn't sure if meeting you yesterday was just some out-of-body experience or was this really happening."

I couldn't blame Kip, but still, time was of the essence. "It's really happening, Kip! You have to hurry. We have to cross the lake Christmas morning, as in now!"

"Because Christmas makes its own sort of magic."

I felt my eyebrows converge. Where had I heard that? The answer was just out of reach, as if it was somewhere in my past. Either way, I liked the idea and though I doubted it, I hoped it was true. However, it was hard to believe in magic while I stared at the blemish on his handsome face. It was handsome, even after last night, I had to admit to myself that Kip Turner was very handsome, gorgeous in fact.

There was something else, something bothering me. I couldn't quite put my finger on it, but whatever it was it covered my body in gooseflesh, and it had nothing to do with the cold. "Kip, please go get your son and mother. We have to go, now!"

He stretched his ungloved hand out to my face. His hand was so cold, I pulled away. On his finger was blood. Instantly, my hand went to my face. It was another nosebleed. I hadn't even noticed. I was so cold, I was close to numb. "Shit," I muttered, wiping my bloody nose on my coat sleeve.

I froze in place as he put his finger in his mouth and sucked it clean like he had just finished eating chicken wings. His gesture was so much like my nightmare it wobbled my legs. "That's really gross," I gasped. The sound of my voice helped to keep me standing. I was beyond relieved that I still had a voice and the strange déjà vu moment from last night ended there.

It was as if I had jinxed myself. As soon as I released the breath I had been holding, Kip smiled and smiled and smiled until his lips stretched so wide his face cracked at the weakest point over the birthmark on his cheek. I pinched myself, confused. Was I having some out-of-body experience or was this really happening? I had just repeated Kip's question to myself, and something about that made the world tilt.

I pinched myself again, this time until I let out a squeal of pain. This couldn't be happening, could it? Kip was picking at his face along the fault line, chipping away at his birthmark like he was peeling a hard-boiled egg, just as he had done all those times by my bedside.

I wanted to run. I think I still could have. I should have darted across the lake as fast as my legs could carry me, but I was too infatuated to pull my eyes away from what was hiding behind Kip's eggshell skin. He had already chipped away more than I had ever glimpsed. The skin under his handsome facade was dark and bruised, taking on a purplish hue.

The pieces of skin were flaking off in bigger chunks now. I could almost see. I slapped my hand over my mouth to smother my scream. Under Kip's face was Jaxson's face, but it wasn't his—not quite—it was battered and bloated, a grotesque caricature of my beloved brother.

"J . . . Jax," I stammered.

"He's in here with me," he said, no longer sounding like Kip but sounding just like my brother.

"With you?!" I shrieked, taking a step back. "Who are you? What are you talking about? Where's Kip and what did you do to Jaxson?!"

"Who am I? I am the family you always wanted, Cookie. *Dear Santa, please bring me a new family that is perfect and will love me forever and ever.*"

I felt my face wrinkle. That was what I wrote to Santa Claus the year Red died. My mother had been so horrible to me before she left and Jax, at first, was no better. Everything was ruined and I wished I had a new family. I did what any little girl would've done and wrote to Santa asking for a new one.

"That's right Cookie, I answered your letter. You wrote your little letter to Santa, and your brother Jaxson threw it in the trash and that's where I found it. Who am I, you asked. You can call me the Christmas Spirit. Santa is a farce my dear Sugar Cookie, but I am real, and I make Christmas dreams come true. I live in the shadow of the yuletide and take the broken dreams of children and give them just what they asked for. As you already know Cookie, Christmas makes its own kind of magic."

My heart thrashed against my ribcage as my mind played catch-up. "I don't understand. You never gave me my Christmas wish. What did you do to my brother?"

"Didn't I? Your mother, she came back that Christmas, having rekindled her relationship with the bottle. You remember how bad it was when she was drinking, don't you? I stopped her from walking back into your life and ruining it."

Silent tears gushed from my eyes. "What did you do?"

He looked out toward the lake, his dark eyes gleaming like gemstones as the sun's rays continued to tease between the trees, casting menacing shadows on the pure white snow. "There are a lot of souls in this lake, Cookie. Ellen is just one of many."

My entire body was overcome with tremors. I twisted my hands in front of me as if I was praying. "And Jaxson, what about him?"

The imposter glanced at his hands where cracks spread over them, hinting at the deterioration hidden beneath. "Jaxson, well, as you know, he needed an attitude adjustment, and he got it."

I could barely get the words out of my mouth; they rolled around my tongue like a marble. "Did you hurt him?"

"He no longer hurts. He's rotting in plain sight; can't you see him? He stands before you as his true self."

My entire body lurched forward as I exhaled my sob.

SECOND CHRISTMAS

"Come now, don't cry, Sugar Cookie. You're mourning a memory of your brother that never existed. It was I who took care of you. Me who raised you. He died the year you wrote your letter to Santa, just like your mother. His death was necessary; it gave me a perfect place to hide where I could stay close to you and wait to fulfill your Christmas wish. For out of all the children I have ever latched on to, you Sugar Cookie, are by far my favorite."

My chest heaved, my breathing ragged as my eyes danced over the nauseating mockery of my brother. It wasn't him, just like it was never Kip at my bedside. He made himself look like that to frighten me. I knew what he really was. I had guessed it all along but was too preoccupied with hating Christmas to make sense of it. Where I could see my shadow in the snow, Jaxson had none. He didn't have a shadow because he was a shadow—*the shadow.* "It was you the whole time, the shadow I saw in the bathroom that reached out for me."

Jaxson's bloated face smiled, his lips oozing over his teeth like slimy cocoons, his gums retreating from yellowed teeth. That was all the confirmation that I needed; his wicked grin told me everything. He was there to terrify me so I would turn to Jaxson—to him—for protection. It was his way of trapping me within my own fears, forever a scared little girl in the same Christmas snow globe. There was just one thing I didn't get. "How could you have known what Kip would grow up to look like? Why him? Why his face?"

"I knew, just as I knew he and his family were what you've always wanted. They're perfect, don't you think?" He reached out and poked my chest with his blackened finger. It burned where he touched me, as if he had just delivered an electric shock to my heart. I stumbled, taking a backstep. "You feel it, don't you?" he asked, his morbid smile stretching. "The perfect man with his perfect son, and for your in-laws, Saint Nick himself and Mrs. Santa Claus. The Turners are the perfect family."

"B . . . but," I stammered, having a hard time catching my breath.

"But what?"

"But they died."

"Yes, they did."

"But . . ."

"Cookie, my dear sweet Sugar Cookie, you are and will always be my favorite, but you still had to pay the price."

My pulse surged. "Price?"

He nodded, his smile plastered to his grim face.

"I don't understand."

"Your life, my dear, and the lives of the Turners."

"They died because of me?" I asked, near collapse.

"They did."

"Oh God, no," I sobbed into my hands, my nosebleed spilling out over my gloves. "I didn't want this. That's not what I asked for."

"It *is* what you asked for. Every year at the start of the yuletide, you get a few days of bliss with Kip and his family, then you have to pay the toll."

I shook my head in defiance, my tears like running faucets. "I never agreed to any of this."

"Didn't you?"

He took a piece of lined notebook paper out of his coat pocket. Unfolding it, he read:

"Dear Santa,

Please bring me a new family that is perfect and will love me forever and ever.

SECOND CHRISTMAS

Love,
Cookie Marlowe

P.S. If you can't make my Christmas wish come true on such short notice, maybe one of your elves can help. I think a few live near me at Kip's Christmas Tree Farm. I will take any help from anyone. Love, Sugar Cookie."

"No!" I choked out.

"You asked my dear, and I have answered."

"You twisted the pain of a little girl who wanted a merry Christmas. Fine, I accept that, but Kip and his family never asked for any of this. Leave them alone. Stop torturing them, let them stay dead. Let them rest in peace, for Christ's sake!"

"Christ doesn't make the rules, I do. Your contract is with me, not him. Once is not enough. I love watching you draw your last breath. Your agony fills me with hope for a happy New Year and keeps me fed until the next yuletide. Every year, for the rest of time, you will die on Christmas and be buried on New Year's Day, a soggy Sugar Cookie." He reached in and pressed his mouth to mine.

I pulled away, breathless. He licked the blood from my nose off his swollen lips, a wide grin cutting across his face that caused Jaxson's putrid skin to crack down the center. The shadow it kept hidden peeked through the gap of rotten flesh. It was like staring into nothing, and with the nothingness came only death. I had told myself when I was a little girl that a shadow can't exist in the light, but I had been wrong. A shadow feeds off the light like a parasite, seeking and destroying, snuffing it out. A moth isn't drawn to the flame; the flame's shadow compels it.

I darted for the lake, glancing back toward the house, hoping the real Kip was out there.

"He'll come," Jaxson reassured as he followed behind me. He was walking, but somehow he was gaining on me. "He always comes."

"Cookie!"

I glanced behind me. It was Kip. He was with Thad and his mother; they were almost to the lake. Kip started to run toward me, leaving his son and mother behind.

"Don't follow me, Kip!" I shouted as loudly as I could, praying he could hear me. "I was wrong, get away from the house and the lake!"

The bang of a shotgun sounded overhead like a clap of thunder. I craned my neck to see Nick dressed in his Santa Claus suit. "No, no, no," I mutter to myself, noticing there was now only one figure standing by the lake. Thad was by himself; his grandmother was already dead.

I watched helplessly as Kip turned around and darted to his son. Another bang. Thad was thrown a few feet, landing on his back in the snow, his blood pooling around him. I looked away, my eyes on the tree line ahead. I couldn't see what came next. I couldn't watch Kip die.

Jaxson, or rather the shadow, was right: Kip and his family were perfect. I felt my brain fog lift, like a curtain being pulled back. Past memories of Christmas with the Turners flooded back to me. I loved Kip and Thad and Emma and even Nick. It wasn't Nick who was brutally murdering his family, it was the shadow that had haunted me since I was a little girl. The shadow was the puppet master, pulling Nick's strings, manipulating his feelings.

My heart ached, the pain the only thing alive in me. I was running away from the pain just as much as I was running away from the abomination that wore my brother's face. I had brought it here to feast on the Turners year after year for eternity in some twisted Christmas tradition.

SECOND CHRISTMAS

There was another rumble-like discharge, and I knew that shot had Kip's name on it. Another followed and I barely flinched. I was next—it was time for me to turn into a *soggy Sugar Cookie*. My guilt was tearing me apart. I wanted to give up, wanted to stop running and just jump into the lake myself, but I owed it to Kip, to Thad, to all of them, to run for as long as I could. They didn't give up and neither would I. If the shadow wanted to see me die, he was going to have to kill me.

I continued to make my way across the lake as fast as I could, the shadow on my heels. I knew I was walking on a frosted mirror and at any moment it would crack.

The sound of the shotgun blast masked the high-pitched whine of the ice breaking up as a zigzag fracture cut across my path. The crack was spider webbing, making a snowflake from Hell on the lake's surface. I pushed forward, hoping to get over the patch of ice before it gave way.

For a moment, I felt like I was walking on water before my foot sank into the ice-cold lake, and I staggered forward. Instinctively, I endeavored to save myself, clawing at the ice for purchase, trying to get my bottom half out of the water before the numbness consumed me.

Jaxson step-stoned the ice until he stood in front of me, my eyes going to the sliver of shadow breaching his skull. "You brought this on yourself, Sugar Cookie. You wanted to know that you were dead as soon as you came back. What about next year? Do you want knowledge, or would you prefer ignorance?"

My grip was slipping. He bent down and grabbed me by my chin, my jaw chattering in his firm hold. My letter to Santa in his hand had cut across my bottom lip, giving me a paper cut that burned in the cold air. It was the only thing I felt; I was freezing to death. "So, what will it be? What will next Christmas bring?"

Kip tackled Jaxson. He was still alive. I was so happy to see him, tears flooded my eyes. Kip reached for my hand, but Jaxson yanked him back, wrapping his elbow around his neck in a headlock.

My grip slipped a little more and my nails slid over the ice in a horrible screeching noise. The letter, my letter to Santa, lay on the ice, just out of reach. I stretched for it, clawing at the edges of the tattered notebook paper. I put all of my energy into propelling myself just far enough to reach it. If I was going down, so was it. I wished I never wrote that stupid thing. All of this death was because of it. It deserved to be at the bottom of the lake with me.

I got it, but it cost me my grip. I slid under the water in an upside-down swan dive. The letter turned soft in my hand as I closed my fist. This was it—I was going to drown. I tore up the letter, wishing there was more of it to rip to shreds. *You have no power over me.*

It was so cold and so dark. The pieces of my letter floated around me like snowflakes, as if it was snowing under the water. There was something else, light coming toward me, blonde tendrils.

"Sorry you drown," Ellen said.

I screamed for Kip under the water, my voice never making a sound. There was only her voice, and it grew louder the further she dragged me into the icy murk of the lake.

CHAPTER ELEVEN
Second Christmas

My eyelids felt so heavy, it was as if they were made of cement. I struggled to open them; something had glued them shut. For a moment I thought I was back in my bedroom, paralyzed without control over my body, then I felt the dampness of my clothes and the cold that came with it. It washed over me in a disorienting pain and that's when I heard his voice. "Stay with me, Cookie!"

The lake—I was at the Turners' lake. I was dripping wet. Ice had formed on my lashes. A shiver went through my body as my coat was yanked from my arms. Warmth quickly surrounded me, followed by the scent of orange, and I wondered if this was what Heaven felt like.

"Cookie, can you hear me?! Come on, open your eyes." My lashes pulled apart, still weighed down by the ice crystals that had collected on them. I was in Kip's arms. He was okay. I was okay.

"Kip, I'm so sorry."

He squeezed me to his chest, and I could feel a whirlwind of emotion stir from deep inside me.

"Thank goodness you're okay. Come on, let's get you inside." He took off his coat and wrapped it around my shoulders before scooping me up into his arms.

"Thad," I sobbed, not able to hold back the pain and guilt bottled up inside of me.

"It's not your fault. You told me it was going to happen, and I left him and my mother unprotected."

Fresh tears of the bitterest guilt coated my ice-encrusted lashes. "Next year Kip, we will all make it. I promise."

I craned my neck, looking behind Kip. "Your dad, Jaxson—where are they?"

"In the lake with Ellen."

My eyes widened. "You saw her?"

"I did. She saved you."

"I thought *you* saved me?"

He glanced down at me with a kind smile. "She saved you for me. She can move on now."

I nodded my understanding. Ellen had finally made amends with her husband. The thing that kept her in the lake—her guilt—could no longer keep her there.

"But Jaxson, he—"

"He's gone. He just crumbled and fell into the lake, and I imagine my father did too. I don't see him."

"The letter," I said excitedly.

A deep furrow formed between his eyebrows. "What letter?"

"The letter I wrote to Santa when I was a little girl. It must have been the thing anchoring him to me—to all of us. He had called it a contract, and I tore it up!"

"What does that mean?"

Kip's question struck me in the heart like an arrow laced in poison. "We're not gonna get another Christmas to save Thad."

His Adam's apple bobbed in his throat. "And what about us?"

"I don't know. We're still here, for some reason."

SECOND CHRISTMAS

"Dad hurry up, breakfast is ready and Grandma said I can't open my presents until after we eat!"

In unison our heads snapped toward the house. Thad had the back door open and was waving to us.

"What's going on out there?" Emma called. "Oh my, is Cookie alright?"

"She's gonna be fine Mom, but you better get a blanket."

"On it. Now hurry up, your father is threatening to eat without us. You know he has the appetite like the real thing."

A smile lit up Kip's face, and I noticed that his birthmark was gone. I ran my hand down his cheek where just last year a shotgun slug had claimed his life. For a second, I thought we were alive, but then I saw the bright silver of his kind eyes as he smiled and knew we had died a long time ago on Christmas morning. "What does this mean?" I asked in a whisper.

He smoothed my wet hair away from my face. "We are getting a do-over—a second Christmas." He pressed his soft lips to mine in a loving embrace. He tasted like the fruit that adorned my favorite Christmas tree. "Merry Christmas, Cookie."

And just like that, Christmas was my favorite time of year again. I knew I would keep Christmas in my heart forever and with that kind of magic, who is to say we can't live after we die?

The End . . .

THANKS FOR READING!

If this book helped you escape, if only for a moment, please consider taking the time to leave a review or star rating on Amazon or whatever platform you use. It would warm the cockles of my little black heart to hear from you.

Looking for something else to read? Don't forget to check out my other books on Amazon.

Follow me on social media (I'm on all platforms under Holly Knightley). Sign up for my newsletter for the latest news, glimpse into my wacky process, and receive the occasional freebie. Stay spooky, and happy reading!

WANT MORE?